The Donkey Rustlers

The Donkey Rustlers is a splendid romp. A riotous and delightful story with a Greek island setting tells how Amanda and David concoct an efficient plot to outwit the unpleasant local mayor and help their Greek friend Yani. Common sense tells the children that as the villagers depend on donkeys for transport, it would be possible to blackmail them successfully if the donkeys were to disappear.

Told in Gerald Durrell's dashing style with his own particular brand of humour, this story will be eagerly read by older children.

Gerald Durrell

THE DONKEY RUSTLERS

Illustrated by
Anne Mieke van Ogtrop

LIONS

First published in 1968 by William Collins Sons & Co. Ltd
First published in Lions 1971
Twelfth impression February 1989

Lions is an imprint of
the Children's Division, part of
the Collins Publishing Group,
8 Grafton Street, London W1X 3LA

Printed and bound in Great Britain by
William Collins Sons & Co. Ltd, Glasgow

For Andreas Damaschinos,
my adopted godson,
who lives on an island
where this could well
have happened

Contents

CHAPTER I

Melissa

The island of Melissa lies somewhere in the Ionian Sea. It is so tiny and so off the beaten track that very few people know about it. It is a lucky island in the sense that water is plentiful and so the countryside is lush with olive groves and cypress trees and at certain times great areas of it are pink and white with almond blossom. It is visited once a year by a small tourist boat which puts in to the port of Melissa and here the tourists tumble ashore and buy quantities of fake Greek antiquities, which are the local potteries' chief source of income.

The island boasts a small foreign colony which consists of one very elderly Frenchman, who lives in a remote villa and very rarely puts in a public appearance. Rumour has it that he is recovering from an unfortunate love affair but to judge by the number of plump, pretty peasant girls he employs at his villa, he has found the right antidote for his sorrow. Then there are two elderly English ladies who spend their lives rescuing stray cats, doing good works and giving excruciatingly boring English lessons to those Melissiots who wish to acquire a knowledge of the English tongue.

That is, so to speak, the static population, but during the summer months the few people who know about Melissa (and who are wise enough) come and rent crumbling villas in the country where they lie in the sun, bathe in the lukewarm sea and every year become more and more devoted to the island and its charming, gentle inhabitants.

Melissa is really a sort of looking-glass world where the term logic can never be used; on it practically anything can happen, and frequently does.

The Patron Saint of Melissa is Saint Polycarpos. He had once, during his travels in 1230, been blown off course by a sirocco and had been forced to stay in the island until the weather cleared up. As a token of his gratitude for the hospitality shown him, he presented the island with a pair of elderly slippers. The Melissiots, enchanted with this generous gesture, immediately made him Patron Saint of the island, and the slippers (carefully enshrined) became the focal point for every religious ceremony.

In the northern part of the island there is a small village called Kalanero. It is perched up on the hillside and down below it there is a flat, fertile area which is cultivated and which leads to the sea. The villagers get up every morning and go down the hillside – and it is a good two or three miles – on their donkeys to cultivate their various crops. In the centre of the village there lies a large Venetian villa which has been decaying in the sun for the last three hundred years or more.

For a great number of years, the villagers of Kalanero regarded this villa with some animosity because the few people who came to stay there never rented it, and so, while other villages could boast that they had villas which were inhabited by foreigners, the people of Kalanero could not. Then there arrived the Finchberry-Whites.

The father, Major-General Finchberry-White, was the personification of what the people of Melissa think an Englishman should be. He was tall, inclined to be a little portly and always walked everywhere with the air of one who owns the place. But he really *was* a Melissiot at heart. He had an obscure gift – at least obscure as far as the

English are concerned – and that was his mastery over languages. I cannot, off hand, recall the number of languages there are in Europe, but however many there are, he spoke them all with the fluency of a native. So he had the immediate attraction to the local peasantry of an Englishman (of all things) speaking Greek. He had another attraction too; he had lost a leg and had an articulated aluminium one on which, in moments of stress, he played complicated African drum rhythms. When he discovered the villa in Kalanero and immediately rented it for a very lengthy period, the villagers were, of course, delighted. Now they not only had an Englishman living in their midst, but a Greek-speaking Englishman and, moreover, one who was obviously a war hero since he had lost his leg. The village was divided into two schools of thought as to how he had achieved this. One half insisted that he had done it while taking Rome single-handed; the other half were convinced that he did it while taking Berlin single-handed. The fact that he had lost it through getting rather drunk and falling down a flight of stairs in a friend's house in Chelsea had not been vouchsafed to them. But it really was his command of the Greek language that endeared him to them most.

The Major-General had only one ambition in life, and that was to paint, but owing to his leg he could cover only very short distances. This is the reason that he immediately rented the villa in Kalanero. It had a wide terrace which commanded a view of cypress trees with the sea as a background to them. So from this vantage point he could paint. He would set up his easel and paint numerous and excruciatingly bad pictures of cypress trees – which he was under the impression were easy to draw and that, if you put plenty of colour behind them, could be made to look as attractive as anything in the Royal Academy. So, with a pertinacity that I am sure earned him his rank, he painted picture after picture from this same vantage point, to the utmost satisfaction of both himself and the villagers, who, of course, treated him with a reverence that would have done credit to a Rembrandt.

There was also, of course, a Mrs Finchberry-White and two children, a boy and a girl. The wife was one of those faded English women who once must have been very beautiful and was allowing herself to decay very charmingly. She spent her time drifting about vaguely, collecting wild flowers and organising thoroughly disorganised meals at irregular intervals. But of course it is the children who are, as it were, the hero and heroine of this story, David and Amanda.

CHAPTER 2

Arrival

All two hundred and fifty inhabitants of the village of Kalanero were, of course, aware of the impending arrival of the Finchberry-Whites and so the whole village was in a turmoil of excitement and activity. Certainly the most excited person in the village was Yani Panioti; of the same age as the children, Yani had become their particular friend, and from the very start he had fallen deeply in love with Amanda and was her devoted slave. His wiry body was burnt brown by the sun and his movements were as lithe as a cat's. Under his thatch of hair – as black as jet and as curly as wood shavings – his huge dark eyes stared at the world with a disarming limpid innocence, or else flashed with wicked impishness. Now he whistled softly and tunefully to himself as he helped prepare the villa, and his heart was gay because Amanda was coming back to him at last.

So the great, creaking, sun-blistered shutters were thrown open in the villa and old Mama Agathi and her husband, who were caretakers, set to work sweeping up the accumulated winter's spiders' webs and scrubbing the white wood floors, while Yani himself supervised the sweeping and weeding of the great terrace. In fact, it is more than likely that the great terrace got more devoted sweeping and cleaning than the rest of the villa – but this was only natural since it was the General's vantage point.

Then one morning when the villagers awoke, they knew that the great day had arrived, for the *Ionian Nymph* (a small vessel with a list to starboard and a large hole in its bows, which was Melissa's only contact with the mainland) was due to arrive. In spite of its manifest unseaworthiness, the General liked to travel on it for, as he said, each voyage became a nautical adventure worthy of Raleigh or Drake. So the *Ionian Nymph* docked safely in the port of Melissa and very soon Yani Panioti, perched high in the branches of an olive tree, waved and shouted to the village below that he could see the white cloud of dust created by Melissa's one and only taxi as it conveyed the Finchberry-Whites towards Kalanero.

The exuberance with which the villagers greeted the arrival of the taxi in the main square of the village had to be seen to be believed. Even old Papa Yorgo, who (as everyone knew) was well past a hundred, had to be escorted out, tottering on two sticks, to shake hands. The Mayor, Niko Oizus, a circular man with a large walrus moustache who exuded sweat and cringing servility at the same time, was there to greet them on behalf of the village. Even Coocos, the so-called village idiot, with his round face wreathed in smiles, was there and was wearing (as it was a special occasion) the old bowler hat the General had brought out from England the year previously. This hat was one of Coocos's most treasured possessions, next to a goldfinch in a tiny cage which he carried everywhere with him and on which he lavished incredible love and devotion. Gifts were given by everybody. There were baskets of oranges and lemons, handkerchiefs full of eggs, almonds and walnuts and, of course, vast quantities of multi-coloured flowers of all shapes and descriptions.

Yani thought that, if anything, Amanda looked even more beautiful than she had the year before, and he followed her with a broad grin on his brown face as she

ran excitedly through the village, her golden hair shining in the sun, her blue eyes brilliant with excitement as she kissed and hugged everybody. David followed her at a more sedate pace and solemnly shook hands.

'Do you like Kalanero?' said Yani teasingly, as the exuberance of the village died down, and the three children walked back towards the villa.

'Like it?' said Amanda, her eyes flashing sapphire in the sunlight. 'Of course we like it. It's *our* village.'

When they got to the big rusty wrought-iron gates that guarded the entrance to the villa, Yani's mood of excited enthusiasm at their arrival appeared to have waned.

'What are you looking so miserable about?' asked Amanda. 'Aren't you pleased that we are back?'

'Of course I am,' said Yani. 'It's just that I'm worried.'

'What are you worried about?' asked Amanda in astonishment.

'I can't tell you now,' he said. 'I'll meet you this evening down in the olive groves. I've got to go and do some work now.'

'Is it something nice?' inquired Amanda, excitedly.

'No,' said Yani. 'It isn't nice at all, and I want your advice.'

'Tell us now,' David demanded.

'No. To-night in the olive groves where nobody can hear us,' said Yani, and he turned and ran back down to the village.

By the time the children re-entered the villa it had been happily and lovingly disorganised by Mrs Finchberry-White and Mama Agathi. In spite of the most desperate attempts, Mrs Finchberry-White had never succeeded in mastering more than four or five words of Greek and as Mama Agathi was no linguist either, a combination of the two was something that had to be heard to be believed. The General had unpacked – as far as he was concerned – the most vital portion of their luggage, his easel and paints, and had set them up on the terrace.

'Aren't our villagers wonderful?' asked Amanda, spread-eagling herself on the flagstones in the sunshine.

'Very kind,' said the General, carefully drawing another cypress tree with great precision and complete inaccuracy.

'Father, you aren't going to paint *another* one of those awful pictures, are you?' asked David. 'Why don't you paint it from some different angle? And you're getting the trees all wrong too.'

'When my senility requires me to have art lessons from you, David, I shall not keep you unapprised of the fact,' said the General, painting away unconcernedly.

'I think you ought to do things like Picasso does,' said Amanda, 'because then nobody would notice how badly you draw.'

'Why don't you go and help your mother?' asked the General, 'otherwise, with her command of the Greek tongue, I doubt whether we will ever get any breakfast.'

Amanda sighed a resigned sigh and wandered through the great echoing rooms to where her mother, in the kitchen, was endeavouring, without very much success, to explain what scrambled eggs were to Mama Agathi. As far as Mama Agathi was concerned, there were two kinds of eggs: one kind was raw and the other was hard-boiled and dyed red for Easter.

'Mother, you are hopeless,' said Amanda, impatiently. 'Even if you can't learn to speak Greek, you might at least stop confusing her by asking for things she has never even *heard* of.'

'But my dear, everybody's heard of scrambled eggs,' said

Mrs Finchberry-White, startled. 'But *everybody*. Why, when I was a gal, we had them every day for breakfast.'

'There are some interesting little pinky sort of flowers in the other room that Yani gave me,' said Amanda, 'why don't you go and put them in water and I'll organise the breakfast.'

Happy to be released from the irksome burden of scrambled eggs, Mrs Finchberry-White drifted out of the kitchen to add the flowers to her collection, while Amanda with a few quick decisive phrases organised the sort of breakfast that the General desired.

Presently the table was laid on the terrace and the General, smelling strongly of turpentine, took his place at the head of it and devoured great mountains of sunset-gold scrambled eggs, huge brown pieces of toast dripping with butter and covered thickly with a layer of the special marmalade that he had brought out with him for the purpose.

'What are you children going to do to-day?' inquired Mrs Finchberry-White.

'I want to go out to Hesperides,' said Amanda.

'No,' David said firmly. 'We can't go to Hesperides without Yani and Yani is working to-day.'

'But I want to swim,' said Amanda.

'Well, you can swim, but we are *not* going to Hesperides without Yani.'

It was curious that, in most things, Amanda was the more domineering character of the two children, but on the very rare occasion when her younger brother adopted that tone of voice with her, Amanda would give in meekly.

'All right,' she said resignedly.

The children had discovered Hesperides their first

summer there. It was a tiny island lying off the coast near
the village, thick with cypress trees so that it protruded
from the water like a little furry isosceles triangle. Right
on the very top was a terraced area with a minute church,
such as you so frequently find in Greece, which would
comfortably accommodate a congregation of three, provided no priest was present. Next to it were two small
white-washed rooms in which for many years had lived a
very old monk. He had long since died and although the
Archbishop of Melissa had written to Athens for a replace-
ment, no reply had been forthcoming. So, as the Archbishop had not heard from Athens within two years, he
had presumed his letter had gone astray. He had made a
mental note to write again but had forgotten about it and
so the tiny island was completely deserted. It was within
easy swimming distance of the coast and the first time the
children had swum out there and Amanda had hauled
herself, brown and dripping, ashore, she had seen, at the
bottom of the flight of steps that led up to the church, a
tangerine tree, heavy with fruit.

'Look, David!' she had shouted, her blue eyes getting
almost black with excitement, 'just look! Golden apples!'

David had gravely inspected the tree. 'They're not
apples, you clot,' he had said. 'They're tangerines.'

'Well, we can *pretend* they're apples,' she said conceding
this point, 'and we'll call this place Hesperides.'

And so, from then on, the island became known as
Hesperides and even the villagers had started calling it by
this name. Prior to this the island had never been christ-
ened and had just been known, somewhat unfairly, as
'the island with the monk on it.'

'Are you going out for the whole day, dear?' inquired
Mrs Finchberry-White. 'If so, I'll pack you up a picnic.'

'Yes, we'll go out for the whole day,' said Amanda, 'but don't bother, mother, it's quicker if I pack up the picnic.'

'Good, dear,' said Mrs Finchberry-White with relief, 'because I've got any number of flowers the villagers gave me that I want to press, and your father wants to paint.'

'Yes,' said the General, with satisfaction, swivelling round in his chair, screwing his monocle into his eye and peering at his hideous canvas with every evidence of satisfaction. 'Should be able to knock that one off by sunset.'

'Well, come on, David,' said Amanda impatiently, 'I want to get down to the sea.'

She went into the kitchen and rapidly and methodically packed a small haversack with the various foods that she thought were necessary for herself and her brother. She did not bother to take water, for the beach to which they were going had a spring that burst from the red and yellow cliffs, sparkled briefly across the sand and was then lost in the blue waters of the bay.

Amanda and David walked the half mile or so down the hillside to the beach. It was curious that though both brother and sister were devoted to each other, they very rarely spoke when they were alone together. It was only when they were out with Yani that they became exuberant and loquacious. They walked slowly down the rough track that led to the beach, happy in each other's company and busy with their own thoughts. Amanda's eyes darted everywhere as she made mental notes of the various wild flowers she saw and which she would collect on the return journey to take back to her mother. David watched the brown and blue lizards that scuttled everywhere under their sandalled feet and wondered how many lizards it would take – if all were suitably harnessed – to pull a cart. The air was warm and full of the scent of thyme and myrtle. They deposited their belongings on the beach, took off their clothes and plunged into the blue, lukewarm water.

Both in their different ways enjoyed their first day in Melissa; David found a baby octopus under a stone and they teased it very gently with a stick so that it would blush pink and iridescent green with annoyance and finally shoot off into deeper waters, like a balloon trailing its ropes behind it, leaving a smoke screen of black ink that hung and drifted in the still waters. Amanda found a contorted olive branch that had been washed clean and sandpapered by the sea and then bleached astonishingly white by the sun.

'I wonder why it is,' she said musingly to David, 'that when nature produces something like this, it looks beautiful. And yet when Father tries to draw the same sort of tree, it looks so awful.'

'That's because Father can't draw as well as nature can,' said David, very seriously.

The two children stared at each other for a moment and then were convulsed with laughter and rolled giggling hysterically on the sand. Exhausted by their mirth they lay and drowsed in the sun for a bit, then ate their food, and swam a little more and then drowsed once again.

'Don't forget we've got to meet Yani,' said Amanda, suddenly sitting up.

'Did he say what time?' asked David sleepily.

'No,' said Amanda, 'but I suppose he means round about firefly time.'

'Well, we'd better be getting back then,' said David, squinting at the sun.

They trudged back up the hill slowly, sun-drugged, their bodies feeling rough from the salt as it dried on their skin. By the time they reached the villa, Amanda had gathered a large bunch of flowers for her mother and David had worked out, as well as he could without the aid of pencil and paper, that it would take 6,842,000 lizards to pull a cart. He was a bit worried as to the exact

number for, as he confessed to himself, he was not sure exactly of the pulling power of one lizard. He made a note that he would have to catch one and experiment.

'Oh, there you are,' said Mrs Finchberry-White. 'I was just coming to look for you.'

The fact that she had not the faintest idea as to where the children had gone and that she would have had to search the entire island of Melissa in order to find them had apparently not occurred to her.

'What lovely flowers, dear. Thank you so much,' she went on. 'I have had such a good day to-day. I found three new species just down below the terrace there.'

'What did you have for lunch?' inquired Amanda.

'Lunch?' asked Mrs Finchberry-White, bewildered. 'Oh, lunch. Well, we had something or other.'

'Did you *have* any lunch?' inquired Amanda ominously.

'I can't quite remember, dear,' said Mrs Finchberry-White, contritely. 'Ask your father.'

The General was out on the terrace putting the finishing touches to his painting by adding a virulent sunset behind badly drawn cypress trees.

'Did Mother give you any lunch?' inquired Amanda.

'Oh, there you are, my dear,' said the General. He stepped back and pointed at the canvas.

'What do you think of that, then?' he asked. 'Powerful, don't you think? Powerful.'

'Over powerful,' said Amanda callously. 'Did you have any lunch?'

'Yes, they did,' said David, quietly materialising. 'I checked with Agathi.'

'Well now,' said the General, splashing turpentine in vast quantities all over himself. 'Did you have a good day?'

'Very good,' said Amanda. She glanced down at the olive grove and saw the first greeny, pulsating lights of the fireflies starting.

'It's time we went to meet Yani,' she whispered to David. 'Just go and make sure Agathi's cooked us something for supper.'

'Why don't you do it?' asked David.

'No,' said Amanda, with a certain self-consciousness. 'I simply must comb my hair. It's full of salt.'

So while Amanda combed her long golden hair and put on a frock which she thought suited her rather well, David gravely organised the menu with Mama Agathi; then, shouting to their oblivious parents that they were just going out for a minute, they made their way down through the darkening olive groves where the trees leaned in contorted attitudes as though gossiping to each other, and where every dark corner contained the friendly green light of a firefly passing by.

CHAPTER 3

Malevolence of a Mayor

Under the olive trees it was nearly dark and the children could hear the musical calls of the Scops owls.

'I wonder what it is Yani wants to tell us?' said Amanda.

'I think it's about his father,' said David.

'But his father died last year. It can't be that.'

'I still think it's something to do with his father,' said David stubbornly.

They made their way deeper and deeper into the dark olive groves where the trees crouched weirdly, their leaves whispering surreptitiously in the evening breeze. But there was no sign of Yani and so presently the children paused and stared about them.

'Where d'you think he is?' asked Amanda.

'Oh, I expect he'll be along soon,' said David.

At that moment from behind the bole of a gigantic olive Yani leapt out at them suddenly.

'Watch out!' he hissed. 'I'm the Devil!'

He grinned at the fright he had given them and then said to Amanda, holding out his cupped hands: 'Turn round, I've got a present for you.'

She turned round and Yani scattered from his hands several dozen fireflies on to her golden hair, where they gleamed like emeralds.

'You are a fool, Yani,' said Amanda, impatiently shaking her head. 'It'll take me ages to get them out without killing them.'

'Leave them in, then,' suggested Yani. 'They suit you.

'Who's that behind that tree?' asked David suddenly.

Yani looked quickly over his shoulder.

'Oh, that's all right, that's only Coocos,' he said and then called to the boy to come and join them.

Coocos shambled forward, removed his bowler hat and bowed to Amanda, placed the little cage containing his goldfinch on the ground and then squatted happily down with the children.

'What have you got to tell us?' asked Amanda.

'Well,' said Yani, 'it's about my father.'

'There you are,' said David in triumph, 'I knew it was.'

'Oh, be quiet,' said Amanda impatiently, 'and let Yani tell us.'

'You see, it was not until after my father died,' Yani explained, 'that I discovered he had borrowed eighteen thousand drachma from Niko Oizus.'

'What! The Mayor! Old oily Oizus?' said Amanda

horrified. 'I wouldn't have trusted him in any business deal.'

'Yes, but then he is the richest man in the village and the only man who could have lent my father that sum of money,' said Yani. 'Now, as you know, my father left me the vineyards and the fields and the little house we had. This is all I possess. I have been working it, with the help of Coocos here, for the past year. It doesn't make me a profit, but it makes me enough to live on. But now the Mayor is insisting that I pay him back the eighteen thousand drachma or else he will take my vineyards and my fields *and* my house away from me as repayment of the debt. And where am I to find eighteen thousand drachma? I have a cousin in Athens, and I wrote to him asking if he could help, but he is a poor man himself and he has also been ill. So, unless I can do something very quickly, I am going to be completely ruined.'

Amanda had been bristling like an angry cat while Yani told this story and now she exploded.

'That filthy, misbegotten toad,' she exclaimed furiously. 'That oily, slimy old hypocrite with his pot belly. I have never liked him and I like him even less now. Why don't we go and burn his house down? It would serve him right.'

'Don't be stupid,' said David placidly. 'It's no good getting excited like that. We have got to think things out sensibly.'

'I know,' said Amanda excitedly, 'we could ask Father for the money.'

'That's no good,' said David scornfully. 'You know Father's motto is "never a borrower or a lender be".'

'Yes, but he'd do it for *Yani*,' said Amanda. 'After all, Yani's our friend.'

'If he won't lend any money to me,' said David bitterly,

'he's certainly not going to lend it to Yani. So that idea's no good.'

'We must think of *something*,' said Amanda.

'Well, why don't you shut up and stop shouting and *think*?' inquired David.

They sat in a group and watched the fireflies winking in Amanda's golden hair and thought and thought.

'The thing to do,' said David at length, 'is to get some sort of hold over the Mayor so that we can make him see sense. So he'll realise that it's impossible for Yani to pay back the eighteen thousand drachma all at once, though he might be able to do it gradually over the years.'

'That's all very well,' said Amanda, 'but what sort of hold?'

'I know, his third cousin on his wife's side is supposed to have had an affair with a married man,' said Yani helpfully. 'Would that be any good?'

'Not with a man like Oizus,' said Amanda, scornfully. 'I shouldn't think he cares what his cousins do.'

'No, it's got to be something better than that,' said David, 'and it's got to be something foolproof because if we don't pull it off, we'll muck up the whole thing and make it even worse for Yani.'

'I know,' exclaimed Amanda suddenly. 'Let's kidnap his wife.'

'What's kidnap?' inquired Yani, puzzled.

'She means,' David explained, 'to catch the Mayor's wife and take her and hold her somewhere and then ask for money before we return her. I think it's a stupid idea.'

'Well, you haven't put up any ideas yet,' said Amanda, 'and I don't see why it shouldn't be possible.'

'I don't think it would work, Amanda,' said Yani sorrowfully. 'For one thing, she's very big and fat and it would be difficult for us to carry her, and for another thing, I think the Mayor would be only too happy to get rid of her. And if we have got the Mayor's wife and he doesn't want her back, it's going to be a great problem, because it's a well-known fact that she eats more than anybody else in the village.'

'Anyway, you just can't go round kidnapping people,' David pointed out. 'It's against the law.'

'Bother the law,' said Amanda. 'Anyway, isn't what Oizus is doing to Yani against the law?'

'No,' said David, 'it's called foreclosing and it's quite legal.'

'Oh,' said Amanda, somewhat dampened by her brother's erudition. 'Well, anyway, I don't see *why* we can't kidnap the Mayor's wife. After all, there's practically no law up here anyway.'

'There's Menelous Stafili,' said David.

Amanda gave a little crow of laughter in which Yani joined, for it was a well-known fact that the local policeman was far too kind-hearted to arrest anybody, and in any case over the years he had worked with methodical intensity on the art of being lazy, so that it was with great difficulty one could get him out of bed should there be any dire emergency that required the enforcement of law and order.

'Well, if *he's* the only law we've got to worry about,' Amanda giggled, 'I should think we could kidnap the whole village and get away with it.'

'Yes, but I don't think the Mayor's wife is a suitable sort of thing,' David said gravely.

'I know,' said Amanda. 'We'll ask Father.'

'We won't do anything of the sort. You know he would immediately put a stop to anything like that.'

'I don't mean *tell* him, you chump,' said Amanda impatiently. 'Just find out his views generally.'

'I don't see how you are going to do that,' said David, 'without telling him.'

'You leave it to me,' said Amanda. 'I am more subtle than you are. Anyway, we'd better be getting home to supper now, Yani. Can you come out to Hesperides with us to-morrow morning and we'll discuss the matter further? In the meantime I'll try and find out what my father thinks.'

'All right,' said Yani, 'I'll meet you down on the beach in the morning.'

The children walked back to the villa arguing vehemently, in undertones, about the pros and cons of kidnapping. When they got back they found the big brass oil lamps had been lighted and were casting a pool of golden light through the windows and on to the terrace where the supper table had been laid.

'Ah, there you are, dears,' said Mrs Finchberry-White. 'I was just coming to look for you· Agathi says supper's ready. At least, that's what I *think* she says, because your father refused to come into the kitchen and discuss it with her.'

'With two women in the house,' rumbled the General, puffing meditatively at his pipe, 'I really don't see why it is incumbent upon me to go into the kitchen and discuss the sordid details of what we are going to eat.'

'Quite right, Father,' said Amanda, smiling at him sweetly, 'you just sit there. I'll go and attend to everything.'

'You are an idiot,' whispered David, following her into the kitchen where she was supervising Agathi.

'Why?' asked Amanda.

'Well, you are overdoing the sweet-little-woman stuff,' said David. 'If you're not careful Father will smell a rat.'

'Nonsense,' said Amanda. 'You just wait and see.'

They sat down to their meal on the terrace and ate for some moments in contented silence.

'Did you paint well to-day, dear?' inquired Mrs Finchberry-White of her husband; she had long ago given up all ideas of her husband becoming a true painter and so now discussed his painting rather as though it was an ailment.

'Another masterpiece,' admitted the General. 'This, by the way, is a remarkably good stew.'

'Thank you, dear,' said Mrs Finchberry-White, delighted, though she had played absolutely no part in the organisation of the food.

'Tell me, Father,' asked Amanda, 'if you could paint as well as Rembrandt, what would you do?'

'I should be exceptionally pleased,' said the General.

'No. What I mean is, if you suddenly found you could paint as well as Rembrandt, would you sell your pictures?'

'Of course,' said the General in astonishment.

'Yes, but would you pretend that they were Rembrandts that you had discovered in the attic?' asked Amanda.

David was getting increasingly alarmed and mystified by his sister's somewhat bizarre approach to the problem in hand.

'If I pretended they were real Rembrandts,' said the General thoughtfully, 'it would be illegal, so I should have to sell them under my own name. I *might*, of course, do it under a pseudonym such as Rembranta, for example. But otherwise the whole thing would seem like fraudulent conspiracy.'

'Why are some things considered crimes and other things not?' asked Amanda.

'That, my dear,' said the General, 'is a problem that has been confusing both religious sects and philosophers throughout the ages, so I find myself at this juncture, full of stew, unable to give you a quick answer.'

'I know,' said Amanda, 'the crimes which hurt people, you can understand why they are bad, but there are other things which don't necessarily *hurt* people, but yet are still considered to be crimes.'

'There are times,' said the General resignedly, 'when you sound almost as incomprehensible as your mother.'

'Well,' said Amanda, waving her fork about, 'take . . . um . . . take kidnapping, for example. Providing you don't hurt the victim, would you consider kidnapping a *crime*?'

The General took a large mouthful of food and chewed it thoughtfully while turning the question over in his mind. 'In my considered opinion,' he said eventually, 'next to murder, rape, torture and voting for the Labour Party, there is no worse crime.'

David looked at his sister with a self-satisfied air.

'Anyway,' said the General, pushing his chair back from the table and pulling his pipe out of his pocket, 'why this sudden interest in the more unseemly activities of the human race? You don't, I trust, intend to take up cat burglary or some similar occupation in the near future?'

'No,' said Amanda, 'I was just interested. You always told us that when in doubt we were to ask you.'

'The trouble is,' explained the General, 'that whenever you ask me I find myself in some doubt too.'

With his empty pipe, he beat out a rapid and complicated rhythm on his aluminium leg.

'Henry, dear, must you do that?' inquired Mrs Finch-berry-White.

'Wattusi drum rhythm,' explained the General. 'They always play it before they attack.'

'It's very interesting,' said Mrs Finchberry-White doubt-fully, 'but I don't think you ought to do it at table. It sets a bad example to the children.'

'I see absolutely no connection whatsoever,' said the

General, 'since neither of them smokes and neither of them possesses an aluminium leg.'

'Yes, but when I was a gal,' said Mrs Finchberry-White, 'gentlemen did not do those sort of things at table.'

'I,' said the General firmly, 'am no gentleman. You knew that when you married me and you have spent twenty unsuccessful years endeavouring to convert me into one. I beg that you will desist from this Sisyphus-like struggle.'

The children left their parents wrangling amicably at the table and made their way up to bed.

'I *told* you kidnapping would be no good,' said David as they climbed the creaking wooden stairs, bent and warped with the arthritis of many winters.

'Well, we'll think of something,' said Amanda firmly. 'We've simply got to solve this problem. We can't let that horrible fat Oizus take all Yani's land away from him. After all, he's only got about two acres and it's barely enough to support him.'

'I know that,' said David. 'But I keep telling you, it will have to be a good idea because if we muck it up it will make it worse for Yani.'

'I,' said Amanda with great dignity, 'will think of something in the morning.'

She carried her oil lamp into her bedroom as regally and as beautifully as a princess and closed the door.

'I don't envy the man who marries you,' David shouted as he made his way down the corridor to his own room. Amanda opened her door.

'I shouldn't think you would *get* anybody to marry you,' she replied and then closed it. David tried to think up a suitably cutting answer to this, but could not, so he decided to go to bed and work on his lizard and cart problem.

The following morning the children met Yani down on the golden beach and together they swam slowly out to Hesperides, pausing now and then to dive down to the sea bottom to examine a strange fish or a black sea-urchin that lay curled like a hibernating hedgehog in a rock crevice in the shallow water. They landed on the tiny island and made their way up the steps, leaving black, wet footprints that were soon dried by the sun. On the terrace at the top they spread themselves like starfish round the small well, and then concentrated once more on Yani's problem.

'My father says,' explained Amanda, 'that kidnapping is a very bad crime and so therefore we cannot kidnap the Mayor's wife.'

'This gives me great joy,' said Yani, 'for, as I told you,

she would be very heavy to carry, and she eats like three pigs.'

'I was thinking last night,' said David, 'that none of the village really like Oizus, do they?'

'No,' said Yani, 'as a matter of fact they all dislike him very much. But he's in as Mayor for four years, and so they have got to put up with him. What can one do?'

'If we could do something,' said David, 'that would turn the village against him, this might make him see reason.'

'Yes, but what?' asked Yani.

The children lay and racked their brains. Presently Yani rose to his feet and grinned down at Amanda, lying golden and beautiful in the sun.

'Would you like a drink?' he inquired.

'A drink?' she asked. 'From where?'

'From the well,' said Yani, his eyes sparkling with laughter.

'I don't think so,' said Amanda grimly. 'I've no particular desire to get typhoid.'

'Ah, no,' said Yani. 'Look, I'll show you.'

He went to the well and threw back the great iron lid that covered it. Then he hauled on the rope. There was a splashing and a gurgling and a clanking noise and out of the cool depths of the well he pulled a bucket in which reposed some bottles of lemonade. From under a stone at the side of the well he pulled out an opener, removed the metal cap from a bottle and handed it to Amanda with a flourish.

'But how did these get here?' asked Amanda, bewildered.

Yani grinned his broad and attractive grin.

'I swam over with them this morning,' he said, 'very early and put them down the well so that they should be cool. So now you won't get typhoid, eh?'

'You are sweet, Yani,' said Amanda and her eyes filled with tears. 'I wish we could think of something to do to help you.'

Yani shrugged philosophically.

'If you can't, you can't,' he said. 'But at least you have tried. That shows that you are my friends.'

Amanda drank her cool drink and then lay back in the sun, her mind busy with Yani's problem, while David and

Yani wrangled over the problems of lizards pulling a cart. Distant sounds were wafted out to the tiny island from the mainland of Melissa: the tinny voice of one old peasant woman greeting another; the sound of a young rooster practising, rather ineffectually, his first attempts at crowing; the barking of a dog and then the familiar, lugubrious sounds of a donkey braying.

Amanda sat up suddenly.

'Shut up,' she hissed at the two boys. 'Listen.'

They stopped their conversation and listened patiently for a second or so, but all that could be heard was the mournful braying of the donkey.

'What are we supposed to be listening to?' asked David at length.

'*That*,' said Amanda, with a beatific smile spreading over her face as the last mournful notes of the braying ceased.

'But that was only a donkey,' said Yani, puzzled.

'Only a donkey,' said Amanda. 'You say *only* a donkey? *That* is the solution to your problem.'

'What are you talking about?' asked David irritably. 'How can a braying donkey solve his problems?'

Amanda swung round on them, her face flushed, her eyes almost black.

'Don't you see, you fish brains?' she said. 'We have been trying to think of something that will turn the village against the Mayor, and that's it.'

'But how,' said Yani, bewildered, 'can a donkey turn the village against the Mayor?'

Amanda sighed the short exasperated sigh of a woman who is dealing with the foolishness of men.

'Listen,' she said. 'All the fields of the village lie down below the hillside on the flat country. Now, how do people work those fields and gather their crops and then carry them to the village?'

'By donkey, of course,' said Yani, puzzled.

'Well, there you are,' said Amanda triumphantly. 'Remove the donkeys and you paralyse the entire village and you cannot call it kidnapping, because it's donkeys that you are taking.'

'What a beautiful idea,' said Yani, starting to laugh.

'I don't know that it's a very sensible one,' said David. 'We will have to think about it.'

'I don't know why you always have to think about things,' said Amanda. 'Why don't you *do* them?'

'But what *is* your idea, anyway?' asked David.

'I will tell you,' said Amanda and she leaned forward with her eyes sparkling.

CHAPTER 4

Reconnaissance

'The first thing,' said Amanda, 'is to find out how many donkeys there are in the village. Do you know how many there are, Yani?'

Yani shrugged.

'I'm not sure,' he said. 'I've never counted them. Maybe twenty.'

'Well, we've got to be absolutely certain,' said Amanda, 'because there's no sense in our only taking half of them.'

'I still don't see how you are going to work this,' David said doubtfully.

'Shut up and listen,' said Amanda. 'As soon as we have found out how many donkeys there are, we then organise a gigantic raid so that we can get them all at once.'

'I think you're mad,' said David with conviction.

'Look, if we take them one at a time,' said Amanda, 'by the time we've taken three or four, the rest of the villagers will have become worried and put their donkeys under lock and key. We have to get them all at once, or else it's useless.'

'I still don't see how we can get twenty donkeys all at once,' said David, 'and then, when you've got them, what are you going to do with them?'

'Put them up in the hills somewhere,' said Amanda airily.

'I don't think that's a very good idea,' said Yani, 'because there's practically nowhere around here where you could hide twenty donkeys without somebody finding them. It would have to be a place which nobody would think of.'

'I know,' said Amanda, her eyes shining, 'we'll bring them out here.'

'What, to Hesperides?' asked David. 'I really think you *have* gone mad. How could we get them out here?'

'Well, how do *we* get out here?' said Amanda. 'We swim.'

'Yes, but *can* donkeys swim?' asked David.

Both children looked expectantly at Yani; Yani shrugged.

'I don't know,' he said. 'I've never thought about it. We don't use them for swimming. But certainly, if we hid the donkeys here, nobody would ever dream of looking for them on this island. That is a very good idea.'

'I think it's an absolutely hair-brained scheme from beginning to end,' said David.

'Why don't you try it?' said Amanda.

David turned the idea over in his mind. The more he thought about the scheme the more pitfalls it seemed to possess, and the thought of his father's wrath if they were caught made him feel slightly sick. But, try as he would, he could not think of any alternative to Amanda's idea.

'All right,' he said reluctantly. 'But on one condition, that you leave the organising side of things to me and don't go doing anything stupid. It will have to be conducted like a military operation and the first thing to do is to find out how many donkeys there are in the village. The second thing to do is to find out whether donkeys can swim, because, if they can't swim, the whole scheme is useless.'

'Well, horses swim,' Amanda pointed out.

'I know. But it doesn't necessarily follow that donkeys

can,' said David. 'Now, we must each have our own job to do so that we can spread out. First of all you and Yani and Coocos, if you can get hold of him, will go round the village and count the donkeys. While you are doing that I will work out a plan so that we can discover whether they can swim or not.'

'Why can't we just take one down to the beach and push him into the sea?' asked Amanda.

'You can't do that,' said David, 'because if somebody saw us it would give the whole game away. I'll think up something. Let's swim back now and you and Yani and Coocos can start counting.'

Excitedly the children swam back to the shore and climbed up the hillside towards the village.

Now that he had accepted Amanda's basic idea, David was really getting quite intrigued by the whole thing. It was, he confessed to himself, infinitely more interesting to organise this than to work out complicated sums about lizards and carts. So for the rest of the day David thought and thought of a way of finding out whether donkeys could swim, while Amanda, Yani and Coocos, armed with a pad and pencil, solemnly went round the village making a list of people's donkeys; the interest with which they inquired after everybody's beasts of burden quite touched the villagers.

'It's a good thing,' said Yani, when they had almost completed their task, 'none of the donkeys have babies, for I think it would be very troublesome to get the baby ones over to the island.'

'Bah!' said Amanda, dismissing that with an airy wave of her hand, 'you could always row them over in a boat.'

By the time they had finished, the children had discovered that the village contained eighteen donkeys and one small horse. Five of the donkeys and the horse – they were delighted to discover – belonged to Mayor Oizus.

'Jolly well serve him right when we pinch his,' said Amanda. 'I bet that'll make him sweat even more than he sweats now.'

At firefly time the children held another council of war down in the olive groves. Amanda reported to David the number of donkeys and also, what was more important, where each one was stabled overnight.

'It's going to be a bit difficult,' said David gravely, studying the list. 'I think we could probably get away with nine or ten of them in one night, but how we are going to manage the rest I am not quite sure.'

'Well, next to Mayor Oizus,' said Amanda, 'the one who has the most is Papa Nikos.'

'And he always gets up very, very early and goes down to the fields,' said Yani. 'We might stand a chance of getting them there.'

'Anyway,' said Amanda impatiently, 'have you thought out how we can find out whether they can swim?'

'Yes,' admitted David, with a certain amount of smugness. 'I have thought up a very good idea. You know that river just before you get to the fields, with the little wooden bridge?'

'Yes,' said Amanda.

'Well, if we could sabotage that in some way so that when they lead a donkey across it it would collapse, we would find out whether the donkey could swim and, at the same time, it is not so deep that we couldn't rescue it if it *couldn't* swim.'

'David, that *is* a clever idea,' said Amanda, her eyes sparkling.

'But, how are you going to sabotage the bridge?' inquired Yani.

'Well, I went down and inspected it this afternoon,' said David. 'Actually it is so rickety that it doesn't require very much at all. I think if you just saw through the two centre supports, anything getting into the middle of it will push the whole thing into the water.'

Amanda gave a delighted crow of laughter.

'You are clever, David,' she said admiringly. 'I can't wait to do this. When shall we do it?'

'Well, the sooner the better,' said David. 'I thought we'd go down to-night, as there's no moon, and do it then. Then we can get up very early in the morning and go down there and watch. The trouble is we don't seem to have a saw in the house.'

'I've got a saw,' said Yani excitedly. 'I'll bring that.'

'Now remember, Coocos,' said David, pointing his finger sternly at the bowler-hatted boy, 'you are not to say a word to anybody about this.'

Coocos shook his head vigorously and crossed himself.

'No, Coocos won't say anything,' said Yani, 'because he's my friend.'

That night the children slipped quietly out of their bedrooms and down the stairs. Each creak made them start nervously for fear it would wake the General and bring his wrath down upon them. They finally got out of the house without disturbing their parents and made their way, together with Yani and Coocos, taking infinite and quite unnecessary precautions against being seen, to the little bridge that spanned the rather muddy canal on the edge of the corn fields. David stripped off his clothes and slipped into the brown water and disappeared under the bridge, having posted the rest of them at strategic points so that should the sound of sawing be heard by anyone who might come to investigate, they could all warn him. Then he set to work. In a very short time – for he found the wood was soft and semi-rotten – he succeeded in sawing through the two uprights that supported the centre of the bridge. He then uprooted them and re-planted them in the mud so that, at a casual glance, they looked as if they were still supporting the bridge although in actual fact they were useless. He then climbed out on to the bank, carefully washing the mud from his legs, dressed himself, and then the children made their way back to their respective homes.

The sky was pearly pink and green with dawn light and there were still a few freckles of stars in it when David went into Amanda's room and woke her up. They went and met Yani and Coocos and made their way down in the fresh morning air to the little bridge. Conveniently close to the bridge several large clumps of bamboo were grow-ing, which offered extremely good hiding places from which they could watch the result of their experiment and here they settled down and waited in silence for the first of the villagers to put in an appearance.

It was perhaps unfortunate that the first person to come down to the bridge that morning was Mayor Oizus him-self. He was certainly the last person the children had expected, for normally Mayor Oizus spent most of his time sitting in the local café, while Mrs Oizus did all the work in the fields, but the previous day Mrs Oizus had complained about some curious animal which seemed to be ruining the corn crop and so the Mayor had decided to take the unprecedented step of going down to see for him-self. In order to save himself the arduous task of walking, he had decided to ride on one of his donkeys.

'Saint Polycarpos!' whispered Yani, his eyes wide. 'It's the Mayor himself.'

'Splendid,' said Amanda, starting to giggle.

'Shut up,' hissed David. 'He'll hear us.'

'He's going to be terribly angry,' said Yani.

'Serves him right,' said Amanda. 'That's what my father would call "poetic justice".'

They watched as the donkey, with great patience, considering the weight of the Mayor, plodded down the hillside and clip-clopped its way towards the bridge. It was very early and the Mayor, who was unaccustomed to such physical exertion as donkey-riding at dawn, was nodding sleepily as his mount jogged along. It came to the bridge and the children held their breath. It clattered on to the bridge and David watched in an agony of suspense, for he was not at all sure that his sabotage would work, but, to his intense delight, as the donkey reached the centre of the bridge, the whole thing gave way with a most satisfying scrunch, and both donkey and Mayor were precipitated into the water with a most glorious fountain-like splash, accompanied by a very heart-warming yell of fear from the Mayor.

'It worked!' said David, his eyes shining with excitement. 'It worked!'

'Absolutely wonderful!' Amanda exclaimed ecstatically.

'You did that very well, David,' said Yani.

However, they now discovered two things: that the donkey could swim remarkably well, and soon had itself out of the canal, whereas the Mayor could not swim at all.

'What shall we do?' said Yani. 'We can't let him drown. We'd better go and help him.'

The Mayor was clinging to a piece of driftwood from the bridge and bellowing for help at the top of his lungs, although at that hour in the morning it was unlikely, he felt, that there would be anybody around. He invoked the saints several times and tried to cross himself, but if he crossed himself he found he had to let go of the piece of wood, which was the only thing between himself and a watery grave.

'Yani can't go and help him,' said Amanda, 'because if he sees Yani he'll know, so we'd better go.'

Amanda and David ran along the bank towards the floundering Mayor.

'Don't worry, Mr Mayor,' shouted Amanda. 'We're coming.'

'Save me! Save me!' yelled the Mayor.

'Stop shouting, we're coming,' said David impatiently. They made their way down the banks of the canal and plunged into the water.

'I'm drowning,' cried the Mayor in such a plaintive tone of voice that Amanda was seized with a fit of giggles.

'Be quiet,' said David soothingly. 'You are all right.'

The children got on each side of the portly Mayor and, supporting him under his armpits, they dragged him, dripping and covered with mud and water-weed, to the bank up which he scrambled looking not unlike a rather ungainly walrus getting out on to an ice floe. He presented a sight so comic that Amanda had to go and stand behind an olive tree so that she could laugh, and even David's mouth was not under complete control as he inquired tenderly after the Mayor's health.

'You saved me,' said the Mayor, crossing himself several times with great rapidity. 'You brave children, you saved me.'

'Oh, it was nothing,' said David unconcernedly. 'We just happened to be passing and we heard you shouting. We were just going down for a – for – er – for an early morning swim.'

'It was in the mercy of God that you were passing,' said the Mayor, removing a piece of water-weed from his moustache. 'Undoubtedly the mercy of God.'

'What were you doing up so early?' said David accusingly.

'I had to go down to the fields to see about my corn. It just shows one should not do foolish things. Somebody should have repaired that bridge a long time ago. I kept telling them about it,' he panted, completely untruthfully. 'So now they will have to do something about it.'

It was fortunate that the Mayor's donkey had scrambled ashore on the same bank as the Mayor and was standing grazing placidly under the trees. Amanda and David hoisted the mud-covered and dripping Mayor Oizus on to the back of his donkey and accompanied him up to the village.

'We know two things now,' said Amanda in English, so that the Mayor would not understand. 'One is that donkeys swim and the other thing is that mayors don't.' She was convulsed once more with giggles.

'Shut up, you fool,' hissed David. 'He'll think there's something funny if you go on like that.'

By the time they got back to the village everybody was astir and their mouths dropped open with astonishment at the sight of their leading citizen, caked from head to foot in mud and leaving a trail of water, riding into the main square. Immediately, magically, almost the entire village assembled. For one thing it gave them considerable pleasure to see the Mayor in this distraught condition, and for another thing, nothing exciting had happened in the village since old Papa Nikos, three years previously, had got drunk and fallen down a well, from which he was extracted with extreme difficulty.

The Mayor, making the most of the situation, climbed painfully off his donkey and staggered to the nearest chair in the café. He had realised, as all Greeks do, the good dramatic possibilities of such a situation. He gasped, he fainted several times and had to be revived with ouzo, and was so incoherent at first that the villagers were quivering with a desire to know precisely what had happened. At last, with much gesturing and much crossing of himself, the Mayor told his story and although there must have been nearly two hundred people standing around, you could have heard a pin drop. The entire village, it seemed, was holding its breath, so that nobody should miss a word of this thrilling story. When the Mayor came to the rescue part, the villagers were delighted. Fancy! The children of their English people rescued the Mayor! The fact that, later on, when speculating on the incident, the general consensus of opinion was that it was rather a pity he had been rescued, was not thought of for this brief moment. Amanda and David were the heroes of the day. They were embraced and kissed and plied with glasses of wine and those hideous sticky preserves which were so dear to the hearts of the people of Kalanero. Amanda and David were, of course, acutely embarrassed and felt very guilty, and indeed looked it, but this the villagers attributed to natural English modesty.

Eventually, having been embraced and kissed on both cheeks by the Mayor, who was beginning to smell a bit owing to the mud, they were released by the happy villagers and made their way to the villa, accompanied by shouts of 'Bravo!' and 'Brave things' and similar encouraging phrases.

When the children got back to the villa they found their parents in the middle of breakfast. Having changed, they slipped into their places as unobtrusively as possible.

'Ah, there you are,' said Mrs Finchberry-White. 'I was just coming to look for you.'

'I understand,' said the General, scrunching his way through large quantities of toast, 'that you have just had the somewhat doubtful privilege of saving our Mayor's life.'

'How did you know that?' asked Amanda, startled.

'There are many things,' said the General, 'such as the Facts of Life for example, which a parent is not supposed to vouchsafe to his children and that includes his sources of information.'

'Well, it wasn't anything really,' said David hastily. 'It's just that the bridge gave way and he fell into the water and he can't swim, so we pulled him out.'

'A noble feat,' said the General. 'After all, he is no mean weight.'

'Want some more marmalade?' asked Amanda, in an effort to steer the conversation on to different lines.

'No, thank you,' said the General.

He took his pipe out of his pocket and beat out a rapid tattoo on his leg.

'Must you do that, Henry?' asked Mrs Finchberry-White.

'That's the noise of Wattusi drums when they've failed in an attack,' said the General. 'I remember it vividly. There we were – five of us – holed up in a kopje and they attacked at dawn. Enormous fellows, all over six feet, with zebra-skin shields and long slender spears. The plain below us was black with them – like ants. We fired until our gun barrels got red hot and finally drove them off; that was where I lost my leg.'

'No dear,' said Mrs Finchberry-White, 'you lost it falling downstairs at the Westburys'.'

'I do wish, my dear,' said the General, testily, 'that you wouldn't always spoil a good story by introducing truth into it.'

The General had at one time or another lost his leg in such a variety of circumstances and in such a variety of places that the children now took very little notice of his stories.

David had something else to occupy his mind: a problem which he put to Amanda as soon as they had finished breakfast and were alone together.

'What about the donkeys braying?' he asked.

'Braying?' said Amanda. 'What do you mean?'

'I mean,' explained David, 'that if we have got all the donkeys on Hesperides and they start braying, then everyone will know where they are.'

Amanda frowned over this problem for a moment or so.

'I don't think we need worry,' she said. 'After all, donkeys only bray to each other. It's sort of like one donkey talking to another donkey across the valley, but if they are all together and there are no donkeys on the mainland to talk to, I think they'll be quiet.'

'I hope you're right,' said David. 'Now, let's go down and see Yani and have another council of war.'

CHAPTER 5

The Rustling

The children met at Yani's small whitewashed house and sat out under the vine drinking lemonade. Coocos was in a tremendous state of excitement because his goldfinch had laid an egg, and he was carrying it round carefully in the pocket of his shirt in the hope of hatching it. As the goldfinch had had no opportunity of coming in contact with another goldfinch, the children thought that his chances of success were very slight, but they did not tell him so for fear of hurting his feelings.

'Now,' said Amanda, 'when are we going to do this?'

'I've decided,' said David, 'that we must wait for full moon.'

'But that's not until about ten days' time,' protested Amanda.

'I don't care,' said David stubbornly, 'it must be full moon. We have got to have enough light to see by and we won't waste the ten days because there are masses of things that we've got to do. Remember, we can't afford to make any mistakes.'

'I agree with David,' said Yani. 'I think it's essential that we do it at full moon, otherwise it's going to make the job twice as difficult.'

'All right,' said Amanda reluctantly, 'but what are we going to do in the meantime?'

'Well,' said David, 'the first thing to do is to take some food over to the island to feed the donkeys when we've got them. We don't know how long we're going to have to keep them there. We can't take it all at once, because it would look suspicious, so every day, little by little, we will take some hay and some corn out.'

'Sometimes Coocos can do this at night,' suggested Yani. 'Nobody really worries about what he does.'

'That's a good idea,' said Amanda, and Coocos beamed at her.

'Then,' said David, 'we ought to have some practice runs so that we know exactly what we are doing on the night.'

'Yes,' said Amanda. 'I think that's very important. Otherwise we will get muddled up and make a hash of it.'

So during the next ten days the four of them quietly and unobtrusively shifted enough fodder to Hesperides to keep even the most finicky of donkeys happy for at least one week. They also worked out a system of communication by owl noises, the number of hoots varying with the message. They found the easiest path from the village down to the beach opposite Hesperides and walked up and down it until they knew every stone and every twist of it. They also went round the village again and again checking on where the donkeys were stabled at night.

Then at last the moon, which had been a mere silver thread in the sky became round and fat and rose blood-red from the sea and they knew that the time had come for their great endeavour.

'Mother, do you mind if we spend to-night out camping?' asked Amanda one morning. 'The moon is so lovely now, we thought it would give us a chance to do some moonlight bathing.'

'Of course not, dear,' said Mrs Finchberry-White. 'I'll pack up some food, shall I? And make sure you take a blanket and that sort of thing.'

'Oh, don't worry,' said Amanda. 'I'll organise all that side of it.'

'Where are you going?' inquired the General, adding a touch of purple to an unfortunate cypress tree. 'Not that I am particularly interested, but I feel it might be useful to know in case I have to send someone to rescue you from a shark or something.'

'Oh,' said David. 'We are not going very far. Just down to the beach opposite Hesperides.'

Amanda packed up sufficient food for herself and David, Yani and Coocos and, in order to add a certain air of verisimilitude to their story (and to put her mother's mind at rest) she rolled up a couple of blankets and (on her mother's insistence) a couple of sheets. Then, at five o'clock, carrying their things, the children made their way down to the beach where Yani and Coocos were waiting for them. Here they lit a fire out of drift-wood and grilled some fish while they waited for it to get dark and for the moon to rise. They had decided to leave the fire alight so that, from a casual observer's point of view, it would give the impression that they were still on the beach, and it would also act as a beacon for them as to the exact spot on the beach which was closest to Hesperides. David had spent two days working this out with the aid of a length of clothes line and endless mathematical formulae.

Although the children pretended to be very casual about the whole thing, they were all tense with excitement and Amanda, though she would never have admitted it, even felt slightly sick. Presently the moon, round and as red as a drop of blood, lifted itself over the edge of the sea and floated slowly up into the sky turning gradually to bronze and then to gold and finally to silver.

'Well,' said David, with an air of nonchalance, 'I suppose it's about time we started.'

'Yes,' said Amanda, swallowing.

'Now, are we all sure that we know what we have got to do?' asked David.

Coocos nodded vigorously, so did Yani and Amanda. They had, after all, been practising it for ten days.

They had decided that their first sortie should be directed against the Mayor. This, they thought, was not only fair, but, apart from that, he owned one of the largest number of donkeys in the village. So they made their way up the hillside and crept with infinite stealth towards the Mayor's house. The Mayor stabled his horse and his donkeys in a small shed that lay behind the house and so, while Amanda concealed herself behind an olive tree ready to give the alarm should the Mayor suddenly appear, the others made their way round the back of the house to the stables. The door to the stables was an old one and held shut by a heavy wooden bar, and this caused them a certain amount of trouble. The bar had to be lifted out with infinite precautions against noise and the doors eased open inch by inch so that they did not creak. Then the reluctant donkeys had to be led out one by one and tethered to each other and then finally the horse was tethered to them as the leader. They led the string of animals into the olive groves, where Amanda awaited them, twittering with excitement.

'You've got them!' she whispered excitedly. 'That's marvellous!'

'Don't speak too soon,' said David grimly. 'Now, if Coocos rides the horse, he can take this lot down to the beach and tether them and then come back.'

'As a matter of fact,' said Amanda, thoughtfully, 'that

horse might be jolly useful. With it Coocos can go up and down that path very much faster.'

'Yes, you are quite right,' said Yani. 'It will be a help, and also I think the donkeys like following it.'

So Coocos was despatched down to the beach with the Mayor's five donkeys and the children awaited his re-appearance.

While they waited, David crept back to the Mayor's house and pinned to the door of the stable a large notice, which he had got Yani to write out in Greek in rather shaky capitals, which read DONKEYS OF THE WORLD UNITE.

'That should give them something to think about,' said David with satisfaction, when it had been successfully attached to the stable door.

In a remarkably short space of time, Coocos reappeared on the Mayor's horse and the children continued with their rustling. In a number of cases the job was simplicity itself, for the donkey was simply tethered under a convenient olive tree and all they had to do was untie it and lead it away.

With the donkeys of Philimona Kouzos, however, things were a little more difficult. Kouzos was notorious as being the biggest coward in the village and took infinite precautions to guard both himself and his livestock against the innumerable disasters which – he felt – constantly lurked around him. In consequence, his two donkeys were put in a shed at night, the door of which was firmly closed with a large and ancient padlock. Amanda and David had investigated this and had discovered that with the aid of a screwdriver it was possible to remove the entire lock but the whole process would take some time. So Yani waited round the front of the house in case Ko

should put in an appearance while Amanda and David
went to work with a screwdriver. They were just removing
the last screw when the screwdriver slipped in David's
sweaty hands and he dropped it. That would not have
been so bad but the trouble was that it fell with a resound-
ing crash on an upturned bucket near the stable door.
The children froze instantly and held their breath; in the
still night, the sound of the screwdriver on the bucket
had sounded like the crash of a bomb. Inside the house
they heard stirrings and mutterings.

'Quick,' hissed David, 'let's get the donkeys out.'

Suddenly Yani saw Philimona Kouzos, clad in his thick
woollen vest and underpants, carrying a lantern and a
shot-gun, appear framed in the doorway of his house.

'Who's that?' he quavered. 'Stand still, or I'll fire.'

As Kouzos was as notorious for his bad marksmanship
as he was for his cowardice, this made Yani chuckle. He
uttered a couple of loud moans, and assumed a screeching,
quavering voice.

'I am Vyraclos, Kouzos,' he screeched, 'and I have come
to suck your blood and steal your soul.'

Kouzos, who had always felt inside himself that something like this would happen one day, dropped his lantern
with fright and it promptly went out.

'Saint Polycarpos preserve me!' he shouted loudly.
'Dear God be with me.'

'It is no good,' said Yani, giving a hideous cackle, 'I have
come for your soul.'

In the meantime, Amanda and David had gone into
the stable and were endeavouring to extract Kouzos's
two donkeys. The animals had had an extremely hard
day's work and so were not, understandably, terribly en-
thusiastic about the idea of being removed from a warm,

comfortable stable, with every prospect of having to do a night shift. So the children had the utmost difficulty in getting them out, but Yani, round the front of the house, was giving such an excellent imitation of Vyraclos that he was keeping Kouzos invoking every saint on the calendar. So the slight noise that the children made in pushing and pulling and tugging to get the donkeys out went unnoticed. As soon as Yani saw them disappear into the trees with the donkeys he uttered a few final moans to keep Kouzos happy and followed them swiftly.

So by the time that the eastern horizon was starting to pale into the green dawn, they had assembled on the beach all but four of the donkeys in the village. The four that were missing belonged to Papa Nikos. It was these four donkeys that had particularly worried David for, because of the position of the stable, it was impossible to steal them from Papa Nikos's house. However, Yani had said, somewhat mysteriously, that he had worked out a method of obtaining them.

'I think we've done wonders,' said Amanda, looking with satisfaction at the line of fourteen depressed donkeys and the horse.

'We haven't finished yet,' David pointed out.

'Don't you think we ought to get this lot across to Hesperides?' asked Amanda, 'and then we have only got Papa Nikos's ones to worry about.'

'Yes,' said Yani. 'That would be sensible.'

All the donkeys had been reluctant enough to go out at night in the first place. However, since fate had decreed they should be removed from their comfortable stables and led down to the beach in the middle of the night and forced to stand there, they accepted it with their usual humility. But when they discovered they were expected to

enter the water and swim, their disapproval was unanimous. They kicked and bucked and one of them even broke loose and took the unprecedented step of actually cantering down the beach with the children in hot pursuit. They finally caught him and re-tethered him with the rest. The donkey's disapproval of sea bathing at dawn was so great that it took the children over an hour to get their catch to Hesperides. Once they had arrived there, the donkeys hauled themselves ashore and shook themselves vigorously and sighed deep, lugubrious sighs to indicate their irritation and their disapproval of the whole venture. Carefully the children led them, one at a time, up the steps to the little terraced area round the church. Here they tethered them and provided each donkey with a large enough quantity of food to keep its mind occupied. They then swam back to the shore for their final bit of rustling.

'Now,' whispered Yani, when they were close to the fields concealed behind a clump of bamboos, 'Papa Nikos is working those two fields over there. He generally tethers his donkeys under that fig tree. When he arrives, I'll slip round behind the bamboos over there and create a disturbance.'

'What sort of disturbance?' asked Amanda.

'Wait and see,' said Yani mysteriously, grinning at her. 'I assure you it will keep their attention off the donkeys – but you and David and Coocos must move fast because I won't be able to keep them occupied for very long.'

'You managed to keep Kouzos occupied,' said Amanda giggling.

'Bah!' said Yani, 'that was easy. He's a fool, that one; but Papa Nikos is not a fool and so we'll have to take great care.'

Patiently the children waited and presently, as it grew light and the sun started to rise, they heard the sound of Papa Nikos and his family coming down to the fields. The only flaw that there could be in their plan was that Papa Nikos might not bring down his full complement of donkeys, but to their relief they saw that he had brought all four of them with him. He and his wife and two sons came down to the fields, chattering gaily, tethered the donkeys under the fig tree and then, getting out their hoes, they started to work, turning the soil over.

'Now is the time,' said Yani.

To Amanda's amazement, Yani suddenly produced a large penknife from his pocket and before the children could stop him, he had stabbed himself twice in his bare foot so that the blood ran down between his toes.

'What are you doing?' asked Amanda, horrified.

Yani grinned at her.

'We've got to make it realistic,' he said, 'otherwise it won't fool Papa Nikos. Now, once you've got the donkeys take them over to Hesperides and then come up to the village. I shall be up there.'

He put his knife away and then disappeared through the bamboos.

'What do you think he's going to do?' asked David.

Amanda shrugged.

'I don't know,' she said, 'but he's no fool, so let's leave it to him. Come on, we'd better move closer to the fig tree so that we're ready.'

They crept round the field and concealed themselves in the bushes near the fig tree. Presently, to their astonishment and alarm, they saw Yani come out of the bamboos into full view of Papa Nikos and his family. As if this was not bad enough, he actually called out a good morning to

Papa Nikos, who replied cheerfully. Asking intelligent questions about the crops, Yani made his way along the edge of the field and through the grass towards the spot where Papa Nikos was working. Suddenly, so suddenly that it made Amanda jump, Yani uttered a piercing scream and then fell to the ground.

'A snake! A snake!' he screamed. 'I've been bitten by a snake.'

Instantly Papa Nikos and his entire family dropped their hoes and rushed across the field to where Yani was writhing realistically in the grass. They gathered round him and lifted his head and examined the wound in his foot, chattering excitedly and commiserating and suggesting any number of antidotes, well-known to be useful in the case of snake bite. Yani's screams were so deafening that Papa Nikos and his family had to shout at each other to make themselves heard. This cacophony successfully covered up the noise that Amanda, David and Coocos made in untethering the donkeys and leading them away.

'A hot iron,' bellowed Papa Nikos. 'That's what we need. A hot iron.'

'No, no,' shrieked Mama Nikos. 'Garlic and olive oil. My mother always used to use garlic and olive oil.'

'I'm dying,' screamed Yani. Since he had seen (through his half-closed lids) that the donkeys had been successfully removed, he was rather enjoying the sensation that he was causing.

'No, no, my golden boy,' bellowed Papa Nikos, 'we won't let you die. We'll take you to the village and get a hot iron.'

'Garlic and olive oil,' shrilled Mama Nikos. 'Not a hot iron.'

'Shut up, woman,' shouted Papa Nikos. 'Do you think that I, with all my experience, don't know best?'

'I am dying,' moaned Yani in a most realistic, quavering voice.

'Give him a drop of wine,' commanded Papa Nikos. 'There's a bottle near the donkeys.'

So excited were the whole family over Yani's predicament that one of the sons ran and fetched the bottle of wine without even noticing that the donkeys were no longer tethered to the fig tree. Yani fainted with great realism and they had to lift his head and force a dribble of wine through his clenched teeth.

'I'm dead,' he moaned, coming round. 'I'm dead.'

'No, my soul. No, my soul,' shouted Papa Nikos. 'We'll

take you this instant to the village and cure you. Go and get one of the donkeys to carry him on.'

The sons ran to obey him and then suddenly came to a halt when they realised that the fig tree was donkeyless.

'Papa,' they said, 'the donkeys have disappeared.'

Papa Nikos's face grew purple with rage.

'You foolish woman,' he said, rounding on his wife as being the obvious cause of the trouble. 'You couldn't have tied them up properly. You fish brain.'

'Fish brain!' screeched Mama Nikos indignantly. 'Fish brain yourself. I tied them up perfectly well.'

'Well, they've disappeared, so you can't have done,' said Papa Nikos.

'I'm dying,' moaned Yani.

'Well, we'll have to carry him up to the village,' said Papa Nikos, 'and come back to look for the donkeys afterwards. They can't have gone far.'

'I'm already dead,' said Yani. 'It's useless taking me to the village.'

'No, no, my soul,' said Papa Nikos, patting him gently. 'You'll not die.'

The four of them lifted Yani up and trudged wearily back to the village with him, Yani assuring them every step of the way that they might just as well put him down under an olive tree and leave him to die as there was no hope for him.

At length, panting and exhausted, they reached the main square of the village, where people were just starting to come to life. Two tables in the café were hastily put together and Yani was laid upon them. Immediately, practically the entire village gathered round. Even Papa Yorgo (well over a hundred as you will remember) tottered out to give his advice, which was listened to respectfully as he was the oldest inhabitant and should therefore have had more experience with snake bite than anybody else. Everybody talked at once. Everybody contradicted everybody else and the whole scene took on such mammoth proportions that Yani was hard pressed not to laugh. Eventually, after his foot had been anointed with seventeen different remedies and bound up in a piece of most unhygienic cloth, he was carried reverently down to his house and put to bed. They closed the shutters and door firmly to keep out every breath of fresh air, for it was well known that fresh air was the worst thing you could have in the case of illness and then, stridently arguing, they made their way back to the village and in the gloom of his little room Yani lay on his bed and laughed until the tears poured down his cheeks.

CHAPTER 6

Panic

Never had the village of Kalanero known such a day as this. The villagers returned to the village, still chattering excitely over Yani's snake bite and they were just beginning to disperse and go their separate ways when into the village square ran Philimona Kouzos with a face the colour of putty.

'All of you! All of you!' he yelled dramatically. 'Witchcraft! Witchcraft!'

He collapsed at one of the café tables and began to sob dramatically. 'Witchcraft!'

The word riveted the villagers as no other word could. Even Papa Yorgo (well over a hundred as you will recall) had to drink two ouzos in swift succession. The villagers gathered round the sobbing Kouzos.

'Tell us, Philimona Kouzos,' they begged, 'what is this witchcraft that you are speaking of?'

Kouzos lifted a tear-stained face.

'Last night,' he said between sniffs, 'late at night, I heard a noise outside my house. Now I am, as you know, a man of extreme courage.'

So fascinated were the villagers by his story that they did not greet this palpable falsehood with the roar of derisive laughter that would have been normal in the circumstances.

'Taking my gun and lantern,' continued Kouzos, wiping his nose on his sleeve, 'I walked out into the night.'

The villagers gasped and crossed themselves.

'Suddenly,' said Kouzos, 'from behind a tree something leapt out.'

'What was it, Philimona?' inquired Papa Yorgo in a quavering voice.

Kouzos lowered his voice to a thrilling whisper.

'It was Vyraclos,' he hissed dramatically.

There was a rustle of indrawn breath from the crowd which now surrounded Kouzos. Kouzos had actually *seen* Vyraclos!

'What did he look like? What did he look like?' they asked.

'He looked,' said Kouzos, drawing on his imagination, 'like a goat with man's form, only with the face of a snarling dog and with two great horns. Also he had a long tail with a fork at the end.'

'Yes, yes,' agreed Papa Yorgo, nodding his head. 'That's

Vyraclos all right. I remember an uncle of mine on my mother's side saw him once. That was exactly how he described him.'

'He said, "Kouzos, I have come for your soul",' Kouzos went on.

The villagers gasped again.

'Luckily, as I am a good, honest God-fearing man, I invoked our patron saint so I knew that he could do me no harm.'

'Are you sure,' said Petra, who was the village cynic, 'that you didn't take a little too much wine last night, Philimona?'

Philimona drew himself up with dignity.

'I was *not* drunk,' he said coldly, 'and there's more to come.'

More to come? The villagers could hardly contain themselves. This was, without doubt, one of the most exciting things that had ever happened in Kalanero.

'What more is there?' they clamoured eagerly.

'This morning,' said Kouzos, 'when I went out to get my donkeys, I found that the lock – that fine big one belonging to my father – had been wrenched from the door as if by a gigantic hand, and my donkeys had vanished.'

'Vanished?' asked the villagers.

'Vanished,' said Kouzos. 'And now I am a ruined man.'

He burst into tears once again and started hammering his fists on the table.

'Vyraclos has ruined me,' he wailed. 'Because the good saint wouldn't let him take my soul, he took my donkeys instead.'

'Are you sure,' asked Petra, 'that they haven't just wandered into the olives?'

'Do you think I haven't searched?' screamed Kouzos.

'Everywhere I have been searching. They have disappeared without trace.'

The villagers looked at each other uneasily, for what with Yani's snake bite and one thing and another, they all realised that none of them had checked on their donkeys as yet. Immediately the crowd melted away as they all hurried home to see if their donkeys were safe. But within half an hour they were back in the village square and the clamour of horror and indignation had to be heard to be believed as the villagers all tried to tell the story of their missing donkeys at once.

'Undoubtedly witchcraft,' said Papa Yorgo. 'This is where we need the help of the church. Go and wake up Father Nicodemus.'

Father Nicodemus never got out of bed much before twelve o'clock and led a fairly blameless existence. He had spent seventy-five years in the Greek Orthodox Church without having done anything more strenuous than comb his beard and sip the odd ouzo. Now here he was, being hauled out of bed ignominiously, and being forced to give spiritual advice to his parishioners at what

amounted, as far as he was concerned, to dawn. By the time the situation had been explained to him by the villagers his head was aching so much that he was forced to have a glass of wine, although it was so early in the morning.

'What can we do?' asked Papa Yorgo.

'Exorcise,' shouted a voice from the crowd.

'What are you going to exorcise?' inquired Papa Yorgo. 'The donkeys have gone.'

'But if we exorcise the place where they were,' said Mama Agathi, shrilly, 'then maybe Vyraclos will bring them back.'

Father Nicodemus could not help feeling that there was a flaw somewhere in Mama Agathi's logic, but he could not put his finger on it.

'I am not altogether sure,' he said, 'how one *does* exorcise.'

'You are a priest, aren't you?' asked Papa Nikos, who had returned from a fruitless endeavour to find his own donkeys. 'You should know how to exorcise.'

'I think,' said Father Nicodemus, prevaricating wildly, 'I think I have it written down somewhere.'

He tottered back to his house and returned with two impressive sheets of paper, one of which was a peroration which he normally gave on saints' days, and the other was a list of groceries which he wanted from Melissa, but the villagers were not to know this.

Never in his whole career had he spent such an exhausting two hours. With a candle and incense he was forced to exorcise each and every stable or the place where the donkeys had been tethered. It was not until they reached the Mayor's house that they became aware of the fact that the Mayor, who was also used to sleeping late, was un-

aware of the catastrophe that had overtaken the village. As soon as he was apprised of the facts, he rushed round to his own stable and there, to his horror, he found that his donkeys and his horse had been taken as well. Father Nicodemus was in full swing with the incense when the Mayor discovered the notice saying DONKEYS OF THE WORLD UNITE.

'Communists,' gasped Mayor Oizus, growing pale. 'It's Communists.' He tore down the notice and read it out in a trembling voice to the villagers.

'We must have a meeting of the council immediately,' he said.

The council of four, with the Mayor as Chairman, met in the village square and the entire population of Kalanero gathered round to listen to their deliberations and interfere in a helpful sort of way.

'I'm sure it's witchcraft,' said Papa Nikos. 'I remember hearing about a very similar case in Cephalonia many years ago.'

'Don't be foolish,' said the Mayor, pointing at the notice which he had put on the table in front of him. 'It's obviously Communists. Who else would ask donkeys to unite? In any case, it's a well-known thing that Vyraclos can't write.'

'That's very true, very true,' said Father Nicodemus, who could see that if he did not steer the villagers away from the witchcraft theory he was going to have a very hectic time from then on.

'Yes,' agreed Papa Yorgo, 'it is indeed well known that Vyraclos can't write, so therefore I suppose it must be Communists.'

'But why would they do it?' queried the Mayor plaintively. 'Why would they take our donkeys?'

They sat and mused on this baffling problem for some moments.

'It must be a plot,' said Papa Nikos suddenly. 'It's a plot to undermine the agriculture of the village.'

'How do you mean?' asked the Mayor, mystified.

'It's obvious, isn't it?' asked Papa Nikos. 'Without our donkeys, we can't gather our food and therefore we are ruined. It's a typical Communist plot.'

'I'm sure he's right,' agreed Father Nicodemus.

'It's possible,' said the Mayor doubtfully. 'It's possible, I suppose.'

'Maybe it's not just this village,' said Papa Yorgo. 'Maybe they've done it to every village in the island in order to undermine the economy of Melissa. It's a well-known fact that Communists do dastardly deeds like this.'

Even the Mayor was a bit shaken at the thought of every donkey in the whole island of Melissa being spirited away by the Communists.

'Well, what are we going to do?' said Papa Nikos.

'Yes, yes,' clamoured the villagers. 'What are we going to do?'

The Mayor looked round him helplessly. Never during his term of office had he been faced with such a problem.

'You're the Mayor,' said Papa Nikos. 'You think of something.'

The Mayor knew that he had never been particularly popular and, in fact, had only been elected to office because all four members of the council owed him money. He could see that by now the villagers, panic-stricken, were working themselves into an ugly mood and he sweated more than he had ever sweated in his life before.

'Where,' he asked, 'is Menelous Stafili?'

'In bed,' said Papa Nikos, surprised that the Mayor should not have realised this.

'Well, go and get him,' said the Mayor. 'This is obviously a case for the law.'

Presently Menelous Stafili shambled into the square doing up the buttons on his uniform and rubbing the sleep from his eyes. The whole dreadful plot was explained to him by the Mayor, four council members and two hundred villagers. When he had grasped the essentials, which took some time for he was never at his brightest at that hour of the morning, Menelous Stafili looked at the Mayor.

'Well, Mr Mayor, what do you intend to do?' he asked.

'You lunatic,' snarled the Mayor, going red in the face.

'What do you think I got you out of bed for? You're the policeman. It's up to you to suggest something.'

Menelous Stafili scratched his head. He had never received promotion, for the simple reason that he had never succeeded in arresting anybody. Apart from that, crime in Kalanero was not exactly on a grand scale. Now, faced with this major felony, Menelous Stafili felt exactly as the Mayor did.

'I suppose,' he said at last, 'that we ought to send a telegram to Athens.'

'Fool!' roared Papa Nikos. 'What do you think Athens can do?'

'It would be more to the point,' said the Mayor, 'if the matter was reported to the Chief of Police in Melissa. It's well known that Prometheous Steropes is a man of most astute mind.'

'Quite right,' agreed Papa Nikos. 'I agree with you entirely. I think that Menelous Stafili as representative of the law in our village, and you as our Mayor, ought to go personally and report the matter to him.'

'Certainly,' said the Mayor, and smiled a smug smile of satisfaction.

'But how are we going to get there?' asked Menelous Stafili. 'We haven't anything to ride on.'

The look of smug satisfaction on the Mayor's face disappeared in an instant.

'I would suggest, then,' he said hurriedly, 'that Menelous Stafili goes on foot and then reports back to us.'

'No,' said Papa Nikos grimly, 'I think you both ought to go on foot and then report back to *us*.'

'Yes,' growled the villagers. 'Yes, that's a very sensible decision.'

So the Mayor, seeing that he was cornered, dressed himself up in his best town suit and Menelous Stafili dismally gave a perfunctory shine to his leggings and they set off towards Melissa.

It was a good ten-mile walk, and whoever had built the road had done it in a rather vague manner, so that it wound to and fro and up and down. The white dust lay on it like a thick layer of talcum powder and the hot sun beat down like a blast furnace. The Mayor and Menelous

Stafili tramped on getting dustier and dustier and hotter and hotter with each passing mile. Never in their lives had the usefulness of a donkey been brought home to them so forcibly. At length, half-dead from exhaustion, they staggered into the outskirts of Melissa. They immediately went to the nearest café, revived themselves with suitable quantities of ouzo, and then made their way to the Central Police Station where Inspector Prometheous Steropes had his office.

Inspector Prometheous Steropes took his job very

seriously. He was an ambitious man and it annoyed him that there was so little crime in Melissa, for he felt quite sure that, given suitable opportunities, he could display a brilliance for detection which would dazzle his superiors in Athens and earn him swift promotion. However, as it was, his superiors in Athens hardly deigned to acknowledge his existence.

One of his most prized possessions was a set of Sherlock Holmes stories, in handsome red morocco binding, which Major-General Finchberry-White had brought out for him the previous year, and which he had studied assiduously until he knew the 'master's' methods by heart.

He was a tall, lanky man with a long chin as blue and as polished as a gun barrel and a sweeping nose that, he liked to think, made him the very personification of his favourite detective. When he was told that Mayor Oizus and Menelous Stafili, in a pitiable condition, were asking to see him, he was considerably mystified, for he knew Kalanero to be one of the most law-abiding villages on the island. What, he wondered, could they possibly want to see him about? The two still-perspiring men were ushered into his office where the Chief Inspector, in his immaculate uniform, was sitting behind his big oak desk, endeavouring to look as much as possible like Sherlock Holmes interviewing a client. He rose to his feet and gave a little bow.

'Mayor Oizus,' he said, 'Menelous Stafili. Please be seated.'

The Mayor and Menelous Stafili sank gasping into chairs.

'It would appear,' said the Chief Inspector, fixing them with a gimlet eye, 'that you have walked here.'

'We have indeed,' said the Mayor, mopping his face with his handkerchief. 'I never realised what a great distance it was before.'

The Chief Inspector mused for a moment.

'Why,' he asked, 'didn't you come on a donkey?'

'That's exactly what we've come to see you about,' said the Mayor. 'We have no donkeys.'

The Chief Inspector frowned. 'What do you mean, you have no donkeys?' he inquired. 'Kalanero was full of donkeys the last time I saw it. You yourself, if I remember right, possess five.'

'But that's just the point,' wailed the Mayor. 'We none of us possess donkeys any more. The Communists have taken them.'

The Inspector started.

'The Communists,' he said incredulously. 'What foolish talk is this?'

'Last night,' explained the Mayor, 'some dastardly Communists came to our village and stole all our donkeys and my little horse.'

'Mayor Oizus,' said the Inspector, grimly, 'can it be that you are drunk, or that you have taken leave of your senses?'

'No, no,' said Menelous Stafili, 'what he says is perfectly true, Inspector. All the donkeys and his little horse have vanished.'

The Inspector picked up a long curved pipe from his desk and tapped it thoughtfully against his teeth, and then rasped it on his tiny black moustache.

'What,' he asked cunningly, 'would Communists want with donkeys?'

'It's a plot,' said the Mayor breathlessly. 'It's a plot to undermine the agriculture of Kalanero. It's probably only the beginning of a gigantic conspiracy to undermine the agriculture of the whole island.'

The Inspector was visibly impressed by this.

'It could be that you are right,' he said. 'But why are you so certain that it's Communists?'

'Read this,' said the Mayor dramatically, as he slapped the poster saying DONKEYS OF THE WORLD UNITE on the Inspector's desk.

'Aha!' said the Inspector, delighted. 'A clue!'

He picked up an enormous magnifying glass and carefully inspected the poster, both back and front.

'You're quite right,' he admitted. 'It's undoubtedly the work of Communists.'

'What do you suggest we do?' asked the Mayor. 'If we can't get our donkeys back, the whole village will be ruined.'

'Don't excite yourself, Mayor Oizus,' said the Inspector soothingly, holding up one hand. 'I myself will take charge of this case.'

He called for his clerk and told him to have three policemen at the ready, together with Melissa's one and only police car, a battered old Ford which the Inspector generally used for trips out to inspect his vineyards. Then, with efficiency that visibly impressed the Mayor and Menelous Stafili, he picked up the telephone and dialled a number. He waited for a moment or so, tapping his pipe against his teeth, his eyes narrowed, looking every inch the determined detective.

'Gregorious?' he said suddenly into the phone. 'Prometheous here. Tell me, Gregorious, you remember those two hunting dogs of yours that you offered to lend me? Well, are they any good at tracking? They are, eh? Would they be able to track a donkey? Yes, yes, a donkey.

No, I am not fooling. I am trying to solve a crime. You think they would, eh? Well, can you lend them to me? Thanks very much – I'll come round and collect them straight away.'

So, with great difficulty, the Mayor, Menelous Stafili, the Inspector, three policemen and two large, friendly and happily-panting dogs, were packed untidily into the police car and soon it was bumping its way along the road to Kalanero, where the Inspector hoped his great day of triumph would come.

CHAPTER 7

The Forces of Law

Now the children naturally knew that the disappearance of the donkeys would create an unparalleled sensation in the village and they had been vastly amused at the villagers' reaction. However, what they had not anticipated was that outside reinforcements might be called in. When they discovered that Mayor Oizus and Menelous Stafili had actually taken the unprecedented step of *walking* into Melissa to see the Chief of Police, they viewed the news with some consternation.

'What do you think's going to happen now?' David asked worriedly. 'If they rope in the whole of the police force they're almost bound to find the donkeys sooner or later.'

'Bah!' said Amanda scornfully. 'That Inspector couldn't find the nose on his face.'

But secretly she, too, was somewhat alarmed by the news, although she would never have admitted it.

'Had we better go and feed the donkeys?' said Yani.

'No,' said Amanda. 'We daren't be seen going over to Hesperides, because if they find the donkeys there, then they'll know that we took them.'

'Yes,' said Yani. 'You're right. I hadn't thought of that.'

'They've got plenty of food to last them,' said Amanda, 'and we can swim out there this evening and feed them again.'

'What do you think the Inspector will say to the Mayor?' inquired David.

'He'll probably come up himself,' said Amanda airily.

'What!' asked Yani, aghast. 'The Inspector *himself*?'

'It wouldn't surprise me,' said Amanda. 'He's always dying to play the big detective and I should think this would be the perfect opportunity for him.'

'Well, we'd better keep a very close watch on what's happening,' said David, 'and we'll all have to give each other alibis if they suspect us.'

'Fancy the Inspector *himself* coming,' murmured Yani,

uneasily. 'It makes the whole thing seem so much more criminal somehow.'

Coocos suddenly burst into a flood of tears. Amanda immediately ran to him and threw her arms round him.

'Don't worry, Coocos,' she said. 'The Inspector won't hurt you. Even if they find out we did it, we won't tell them that you were involved.'

Coocos, however, with a tremendous effort to overcome his speech impediment, explained that it was not the thought of arrest that had upset him, but the fact that he had just discovered his goldfinch egg had broken in his pocket.

'Let's go up the hill where we can see the road and watch for them coming back,' said David, 'because I should think they'll come back by taxi.'

So they trooped up to the top of the hill and Yani climbed up into the branches of the olive tree (where he had watched for the arrival of the children) and the children lay in the shade below. After what seemed an interminable time, Yani suddenly said: 'They're coming! I can see the dust! They're coming!'

He scrambled down out of the olive and the children made their way hurriedly to the main square of the village.

'The Mayor's coming back. The Mayor's coming back,' shouted Amanda and immediately the villagers flocked into the square.

The police car drew to a shuddering halt in the centre of the square with an impressive screaming of brakes and discharged its motley cargo.

'Now,' said the Inspector, patting the brief-case that he had brought with him, 'I must have a suitable place where I can interview witnesses.'

Two café tables were immediately joined together and a white cloth procured which was spread over them. The Inspector took his place at these and carefully unpacked from his brief-case a magnificent array of criminal-catching devices, which greatly impressed the villagers. There was his magnifying glass, a small ink pad and some paper for taking finger-prints, a camera for photographing clues and – perhaps the best of all – six pairs of hand-cuffs. The three policemen had, meanwhile, been busy tying up the two hunting dogs. They then relaxed in the shade and were plied with drinks by the villagers, while they listened reverently to Inspector Prometheous Steropes conducting the case.

'Now,' said the Inspector, 'to question the witnesses.'

'But there *aren't* any witnesses,' the Mayor pointed out, 'nobody saw it happen.'

'But there was this fellow Kouzos,' said the Inspector, narrowing his eyes. 'Didn't you say he saw something?'

'But he saw Vyraclos,' protested Papa Yorgo. 'That was quite different.'

The Inspector leant forward and fixed Papa Yorgo with a piercing gaze.

'And how do you know,' he inquired, 'that this Vyraclos he saw wasn't a *Communist disguised as Vyraclos*?'

A ripple of delight spread through the crowd. What astuteness of mind! What brilliance of detection! Why hadn't they thought of that? The Inspector smiled a small, grim smile, the smile of a detective from whom nothing was hidden.

'That hadn't occurred to you, had it?' he said with satisfaction. 'Bring the man Kouzos here.'

Eager hands pushed Kouzos from the back of the crowd to the front where he stood in front of the table trembling slightly with awe at the majesty of the law.

'Now,' said the Inspector, 'tell me exactly what happened.'

'He heard a noise late at night – ' began Papa Yorgo.

'If you please,' said the Inspector holding up a hand, 'I would like the witness to tell his own story.'

'I heard a noise late at night,' began Kouzos in a trembling voice, 'and being a man of intrepid disposition I immediately seized my shotgun and my lantern and went out to investigate.'

'What kind of shotgun was it?' inquired the Inspector.

'A double-barrel twelve bore,' said Kouzos.

The Inspector wrote this down with every evidence of satisfaction.

'It's important,' he said, 'not to overlook a single fact in a case like this. For all we know, the shotgun might turn out to be a vital clue. Well, go on.'

'I shouted out, "Who's there? Stand still or I'll drill you full of holes",' said Kouzos.

'It would have been very unwise of you to do that,' remarked the Inspector severely, 'I might have had to arrest you for murder. Go on.'

'From behind a tree leaped this – this *thing*,' said Kouzos, 'with huge horns and a huge tail and shaggy legs like a goat.'

'Did it have hooves?' inquired the Inspector.

'Yes,' said Kouzos eagerly. 'Huge hooves.'

The Inspector made a note of this.

'And then?' he said.

'And then it said, "Kouzos, I have come for your soul and to suck your blood",' said Kouzos, crossing himself.

'To which you replied?' inquired the Inspector.

'Saint Polycarpos preserve me from Vyraclos,' said Kouzos.

'Very right and proper,' said the Inspector. He sat back and pulled his curved pipe out of his pocket and tapped it thoughtfully against his teeth.

'It was obviously a good disguise,' he said at last. 'Otherwise you would have *known* it was a Communist. Wouldn't you?'

'But of course,' agreed Kouzos. 'My family have always been well known for their eyesight.'

'Well now,' said the Inspector, 'the first thing to do is to go and examine the place where you saw it.'

Picking up his magnifying glass he strode off towards Kouzos's house, closely followed by the entranced villagers of Kalanero.

The way he had conducted the case so far had fascinated the children. Indeed, Amanda was hard put not to have a fit of giggles. When the Inspector, accompanied by the entire village, got to Kouzos's house, he clenched his pipe between his teeth and surveyed the area majestically.

'Whereabouts,' he inquired of Kouzos, 'did you see it?'

'Just there,' said Kouzos, pointing to an area beneath the olives on which were standing some one hundred and fifty villagers.

'Fools!' roared the Inspector. 'Get back! You're standing all over the clues!'

Hurriedly the villagers retreated and the Inspector, with great care, got down on his knees and with his magnifying glass examined a large area beneath the olive tree, making little grunting noises to himself periodically. The villagers stood and whispered among themselves about how brilliant the Inspector was, how you could see it from the way he was conducting the case and how they were absolutely positive that if anybody could get their donkeys back, he could. Presently the Inspector got to his feet and dusted his knees.

'There are no footprints,' he said, with every evidence of satisfaction, and made a note of it in his book.

'How does he expect to find footprints?' whispered David to Amanda. 'The ground is as dry as a bone.'

'If we'd only thought of it,' said Amanda, 'we could have put some there for him.'

The Inspector stalked back to the village and sat down once again at the table.

'Now,' he said. 'This case has some very curious aspects. Very curious indeed. However, rest assured that I will leave no stone unturned in my endeavours to capture these Communists and have your donkeys returned to you. I, Prometheous Steropes, promise you this.'

There was a murmur of approval from all the villagers.

'I have brought with me, as you will see,' continued the Inspector, pointing proudly at the two mongrels who were panting under the café table, 'two extremely fine tracking dogs and with their aid we should have no difficulty at all in tracing the whereabouts of the donkeys. However, as it is more than likely that the Communists will be with the donkeys when we locate them, I would like to ask for six volunteers to come with me and my men in case the robbers should put up a fight for it, or, indeed, in case they should outnumber us.'

Six young men of the village stepped forward eagerly. There was no shortage of volunteers. Indeed, from the

general surge forward, it appeared that everybody in the
village wanted to volunteer. However, the Inspector took
the six young men. They felt very proud and happy because they knew now that whenever they walked down
the street, the people would say, 'Do you see him? He's
one of the people who caught the Communists who stole
our donkeys.'

'Now,' said the Inspector, 'the first thing to do is to give
the dogs a scent. Mr Mayor, would you be so good as to
lend me one of your saddle-cloths which we can give to
the dogs to sniff?'

Mayor Oizus sent his youngest son running off to his
house and he returned bearing a gaudy piece of woven
cloth. This the Inspector proceeded to wave under the
noses of the two dogs, who sniffed at it, sneezed violently
and then sat there panting and wagging their tails.

'They sneezed,' said the Inspector with satisfaction.
'That shows they've got the scent.'

He untied the two dogs and, holding on to their leash,
proceeded through the village with them, followed by
Menelous Stafili, the three policemen from Melissa and
the six village boys. The villagers let them get a hundred
yards or so ahead and then followed *en masse*.

The dogs had at first looked upon the whole afternoons'

outing as being rather enjoyable. They had liked riding in the car, for example, although one of them had got so excited that he had been sick on a policeman. But they had been sitting for a long time in the hot sun under the café table, and so now were not unnaturally somewhat bored. Yet here was the kind Inspector willing to take them for a walk. They were delighted. They put their noses to the ground and sniffed all the lovely smells that dogs can smell and frequently dragged the Inspector to one side so that they could cock their leg on a doorway. They sniffed and snuffled round and round in a circle.

'I think they've got the scent,' said the Inspector excitedly.

By this time they had left the village and were some distance into the olive groves. The dogs cast about in a circle whining and wagging their tails vigorously, and suddenly they both set off in the same direction.

'Forward, men!' cried the Inspector. 'They're hot on the track.'

The dogs were now straining eagerly at the leash and the Inspector was having to run to keep up with them and his gallant band of men ran behind him. The dogs ran through the olive groves in a wide circle and then re-entered the village. They dragged the panting Inspector back through the main square, down several side turnings, up the flight of steps by the village well and then, to the astonishment of everybody (not least the Inspector) they rushed to the door of the Mayor's house and started scratching at it and whining and wagging their tails delightedly. The Mayor grew pale. He had heard of miscarriages of justice and he could see that if the dogs were taken as evidence, he was going to be implicated in the

donkey-stealing plot. The Inspector frowned as he watched the dogs scratching at the door.

'Tell me, Mayor Oizus,' he inquired, 'why should the dogs have led me to your house?'

'I have absolutely no idea,' said the Mayor, sweating. 'I assure you, I have absolutely no idea whatsoever.'

'Don't be silly,' said Mrs Oizus suddenly. 'Don't you know our bitch is in season?'

A roar of laughter from the assembled villagers greeted this statement and the Inspector flushed a dark red.

'You should have told me that before,' he said curtly. 'It could almost have been described as obstructing the law in the execution of its duty.'

'I am very sorry, Inspector,' said Mayor Oizus, casting a malevolent look at his wife. 'But I was unaware of this.'

'Well,' said the Inspector, 'we will have to try again. We'll take them farther away from the village where there won't be so many distractions.'

So they set off through the olive groves until they were a quarter of a mile or so away from the village and then once more the dogs were made to sniff the donkey's saddle-cloth. Having been deprived of paying a social call on a bitch in such an interesting condition, the dogs philosophically accepted what they imagined to be an ordinary hunting trip. On these (with their own master) they were used to wandering blindly about the countryside until they stumbled upon a hare or flushed a woodcock from under an olive tree, and they could see no reason for varying their performance for the sake of the Inspector. They led him and his men up and down the hillsides, in and out of cane brakes and across small streams, sniffing and wagging their tails, thus giving their human companions constant encouragement. It was not

long before they approached a very steep and stony hillside where the Inspector missed his footing and fell into a
gully, grazing his shin badly and breaking his magnifying
glass. It was here he decided that it would be best to let the
dogs off the leash.

It was, as it turned out, an extremely unwise thing to
do. Within a very short space of time, the Inspector and
his men had lost all contact with the dogs, and, spreading
out in search of them, soon lost all contact with each
other as well. The dogs continued gaily over the hills and
then, finding that their human companions were not,
apparently, any longer interested in the hunt – since they
had not joined them – they decided to cut back to the
village and pay the social call on the Mayor's bitch that
they had been deprived of earlier.

Gradually it grew dark and the villagers of Kalanero
started to get worried. First the dogs had arrived back,
closely followed by Menelous Stafili, who said he had lost
all contact with the main body and, as he was not pre-
pared to arrest an unknown quantity of Communists
single-handed, he had thought it only sensible to return
to the village. Shortly after this, the young men of Kalanero started to trickle in with the same story, that they
had got separated from the main body and thought it
useless to continue on their own, but still there was no
sign of the Inspector and the three policemen from
Melissa.

'What on earth do you think's happened to them?'
asked David. 'I do hope nothing serious.'

'I shouldn't think so,' said Amanda, 'they can't come
to much harm up in those hills.'

'I don't know,' said David worriedly, 'you could fall and
break a leg in one of those gullies.'

'Oh, don't be so gloomy,' said Amanda, impatiently. 'I'm sure they'll be all right.'

'David is right,' said Yani seriously. 'Until the moon comes up, it's very difficult to see on those hills and there are some places which are quite dangerous.'

'Well, what can we do?' asked Amanda. 'We can't go and look for them.'

'We could suggest to Papa Yorgo that some of the villagers went with lanterns to look for them,' said David.

'That's an excellent idea,' agreed Yani, 'because then they'll see the lanterns and know which way to go.'

So the children went to Papa Yorgo and suggested to him that a search party be sent out. The villagers immediately acclaimed the children for their astuteness of mind, and presently a crowd of people with lanterns went off up into the hills and an hour or so later, grimy, tattered and torn, the Inspector and his three men were led ignominiously back into the village. The Inspector sank wearily on to a chair in the café, and the villagers tenderly poured him wine and anointed his various cuts and abrasions, but they could do nothing about his wounded soul, for the Inspector realised that his stock in the village had sunk almost as low as that of Mayor Oizus.

'We came,' he announced, clearing his throat, 'within an ace of success.'

'Yes, yes, you did,' chorused the villagers, who felt sorry for him.

'Within an ace of success,' he continued, thumping the table with his fist. He gulped angrily.

'If it hadn't been for those damned sex-mad dogs and that bitch of yours,' he said to Mayor Oizus, 'we would probably now have both the donkeys *and* the Communists.'

'Yes, yes,' chorused the villagers. 'It was Mayor Oizus's bitch that did it.'

They glared at the Mayor as though he personally was responsible for his bitch coming into season.

'I shall not, however, give up,' said the Inspector. 'I'll spend the night here, if you, Mayor Oizus, can spare me a bed, and to-morrow we'll try again. Rest assured that we'll meet with success.'

'Yes, yes,' said the villagers soothingly. 'Of course you will.'

Leaving the Inspector giving the entranced villagers a brilliant account of one of Sherlock Holmes's better-known cases (which, for some reason, the villagers thought had been solved by the Inspector) Amanda and David made their way back to the villa for supper.

'Ah, there you are, dears,' said Mrs Finchberry-White. 'I was just coming to look for you. Supper's ready.'

Supper was from many points of view a difficult meal. The children were worried because they felt that if the villagers did go on searching, they must inevitably find the donkeys and that suspicion would fall on them, because they were the only ones who ever used Hesperides. Major-General Finchberry-White had spent the afternoon, in between painting, in perfecting some messages of the Congo talking-drum on his leg, and kept asking for things like salt and pepper and bread by this method. As Mrs Finchberry-White could not translate the Congo talking-drum messages, she became increasingly distraught and the Major-General increasingly irritable. However, at length the children had finished their food and they slipped down through the moonlit olive groves and swam over to Hesperides to feed the donkeys.

Of everyone in the vicinity, it was probably the eighteen

donkeys and the Mayor's little horse who were the most satisfied with life at that moment. They had spent a quiet day dozing and munching, and now here were the same friendly children bringing them still more food. What more could any donkey ask for?

CHAPTER 8

Solution

The following morning, to the consternation of Inspector Steropes and the entire village, another notice saying DONKEYS OF THE WORLD UNITE was found pinned to the Mayor's front door. Amanda and David were no less amazed and alarmed than the villagers.

'It must have been Yani,' said David. 'Silly fool.'

'He's got them all buzzing like a hive of bees, anyway,' said Amanda.

But when they went down to see Yani, he hotly denied all knowledge of the poster.

'Well, who did it?' asked Amanda.

They all looked at Coocos as being the most likely suspect and Coocos nodded his head vigorously and beamed at Amanda. He explained, with great difficulty, because of his stammer, that since they had put a notice like that up on the first night when they took the donkeys, he was under the impression that one had to be put up every night.

'Oh, Coocos,' said David in despair, 'you are an *idiot*.'

'Don't say things like that to him,' said Amanda indignantly. 'The poor boy was only trying to help.'

'I don't think it's going to be much help,' said Yani grimly. 'It's got the villagers and the Inspector so angry that I think they'll redouble their efforts.'

And indeed the villagers were angry.

'To think,' roared Papa Nikos, his face going purple,

'that *in spite* of the Inspector being here, Communists are creeping in and out of our village as if they owned the place. Something must be done.'

'Yes,' growled the villagers, 'something must be done.'

'Keep calm, keep calm,' said the Inspector placatingly. 'This morning we are going to have another search. Yesterday we almost succeeded. To-day we *will* succeed.'

But it was obvious from their demeanour that the villagers did not share the Inspector's high hopes. However, with his two faithful hounds and his band of policemen and volunteers, the Inspector spent a hot and sticky morning scrambling over the hillsides all round Kalanero to return, at midday, defeated and donkeyless.

'I'll go,' the Inspector said to the Mayor, 'to see Major-General Finchberry-White. After all, he's a man of great bravery and courage and brain, and moreover he's a compatriot of Sherlock Holmes. I am certain he will be able to give us some helpful advice.'

So Prometheous Steropes made his way up to the villa.

'Good lord,' said David as they saw him approach. 'You don't think he's found out, do you?'

'No,' said Amanda, with a sinking feeling in the pit of her stomach. 'I'm sure he can't have. I think he's just come up to say hallo to father.'

'Ah, my sweet ones,' said Steropes, beaming fondly at the two children. 'Is your father at home? I would very much like to talk to him.'

'Yes, Inspector,' said Amanda meekly. 'He's out on the terrace painting.'

'Is it permitted to interrupt him?' inquired Steropes.

'Oh, yes,' said Amanda. 'It doesn't matter how often you interrupt him, the paintings are still as bad.'

'You shouldn't say that,' said the Inspector, shocked. 'Your father is a very fine artist.'

He made his way out on to the terrace where the General was putting the finishing touches to a sunset that looked like an atomic explosion.

'My dear Inspector,' said the General, putting down his paint brushes and limping forward to shake hands. 'How very nice to see you.'

'If you would be so kind as to let me interrupt your work for a few minutes?' asked Steropes.

'Of course, my dear chap,' said the General.

He took his pipe out of his pocket and beat a rapid and complicated rhythm on his leg.

'Congo,' he explained to the Inspector. 'What they call talking-drums. They send messages by them. I've just been teaching my wife. We'll see if it works. Sit down, sit down, do.'

At that moment Mrs Finchberry-White appeared on the terrace with a large tray of bottles and glasses.

'By Jove!' said the General in astonished delight, 'you've got it, Agnes!'

'Got what, dear?' said Mrs Finchberry-White, bewildered.

'My message,' explained the General.

'What message?' asked Mrs Finchberry-White.

'The message to bring out the drinks,' said the General.

'Oh,' said Mrs Finchberry-White. 'Oh, yes. Amanda told me.'

The General sighed sorrowfully.

'Have a drink, Inspector,' he said.

They sat sipping their ouzos for a moment and the Inspector made polite comments about the General's latest painting.

'Tell me,' asked the General, 'what brings you to Kalanero?'

'Well,' said the Inspector, 'that's really what I came to see you about. I'm here investigating one of the worst crimes of my career.'

'By George! Really?' asked the General.

'Is it possible that you haven't heard about the donkeys?' inquired the Inspector.

'Donkeys?' said the General blankly. 'What donkeys?'

'All the donkeys of Kalanero,' said the Inspector, making an all-embracing gesture with his arms and nearly upsetting his drink. 'They've all been stolen by Communists.'

The General screwed his monocle firmly into his eye and surveyed the Inspector.

'You don't say?' he inquired.

'Indeed, yes,' said the Inspector. 'I've been investigating for the past twenty-four hours without success and so I came to ask for your advice. For, after all, you are a compatriot of Sherlock Holmes.'

'I keep telling you,' said the General with a long-suffering air, 'that Sherlock Holmes is an entirely *imaginary* character.'

'Ah, he couldn't be *entirely* imaginary,' said the Inspector, 'not with such brilliant powers of mind. I intend some day to go to London and see the place where he lived. But, to return to the donkeys. As I have so far met with no success in my investigations (and you can rest assured that I have left no stone unturned) I would be most grateful for your advice.'

The General took his monocle out, polished it carefully and replaced it, frowning slightly.

'My dear Inspector,' he said, 'I come here once a year

for a little peace and quiet in order to paint. During my sojourn I endeavour not to get mixed up in any island politics. The first year they tried to get me to decide whose cow belonged to who. The second year they wanted me to decide whether Papa Yorgo had swindled Papa Nikos out of three hundredweight of olives and the third year they wanted me to decide whether it was right that Kouzos should put a lock on his well so that nobody could drink out of it. On all three occasions I refused to participate, so I really don't see how I could help you with your problem.'

Amanda and David, standing behind the half-closed shutters of the living-room, were listening to this conversation with bated breath.

'That's a jolly good thing,' whispered Amanda. 'With Father helping him, he might get somewhere.'

'But, General,' pleaded the Inspector, 'my whole *future* depends upon you. If I solve this case successfully, who knows, it might get to the ears of my superiors in Athens and I might even earn a promotion.'

The General got to his feet, lit his pipe and limped slowly down the terrace, the Inspector loping along beside him. Amanda and David were mortified, for as their father and the Inspector paced up and down, they could only hear snatches of the conversation.

'. . . and similar cases,' said the General, 'frequently happens . . . I remember once in Bangalore, where I lost my leg . . . However, this is what you should do . . .'

They strained their ears, but they could not hear what it was the General was suggesting. Presently the Inspector, wreathed in smiles, took his leave.

The Finchberry-Whites sat down to lunch. Amanda and David glanced uneasily at each other, for their father seemed in a particularly good mood. He kept humming snatches of 'The Road to Mandalay' in between mouthfuls of food.

'What did the Inspector want, Father?' asked Amanda at last, her curiosity getting the better of her.

'The Inspector?' asked the General. 'Oh, he just popped in to pass the time of day and ask my advice on a little problem.'

'Were you able to help him, dear?' inquired Mrs Finchberry-White.

'Oh, I think so,' said the General airily.

Amanda and David gulped their food down and hurriedly left the table. It was obvious that the General was not going to disclose what his advice had been, so their only hope was to stick as close to the Inspector as possible. They ran down to Yani's house and panted out the news to him. Then the three of them made their way to the village. Here they found that the Inspector had called an extraordinary meeting of the village council. Needless to say, most of the village attended it as well.

'Now,' said the Inspector, clenching his pipe firmly between his teeth, 'as I have said before, this case has many unusual aspects. I have endeavoured, as you know, to solve it by the most modern and up-to-date methods of detection. But detection, as you know, is based upon fair play and Communists, as you know, don't even comprehend the meaning of the word. That has been our undoing.'

'Quite right, quite right,' agreed Papa Yorgo. 'I remember once having my entire strawberry crop stolen by a man from Melissa who was an avowed Communist. As the Inspector says, they have no sense of fair play.'

'Quite so,' said the Inspector. 'Now I have decided to try another method.'

'What is it? What is it?' asked the villagers, eagerly.

'I have decided,' said the Inspector, looking stern and noble, 'that we, or rather, that is to say, *you*, should offer a reward for your donkeys.'

There was a gasp of dismay at this.

'But where can we find enough money for all those donkeys?' quavered Mama Agathi.

'I have here,' said the Inspector, taking a piece of paper out of his pocket and laying it on the table, 'I have here a list of all the missing animals, and their approximate market prices. It comes to 25,000 drachma.'

A wail of dismay went up from the villagers.

'But where,' asked Papa Nikos in despair, 'can we possibly find 25,000 drachma.'

'This is precisely the point,' said the Inspector cunningly. 'You don't offer a reward of that amount. You offer a smaller reward, but one sufficiently big to be attractive. It is a well-known fact that Communists like money, and so if we offer this reward, one of the band of robbers is sure to betray the others since, as I say, they have no sense of fair play.'

'This is a very good idea,' Papa Nikos pointed out, 'but we are all of us poor.'

'Yes, yes,' agreed the Mayor hurriedly, 'we are all of us poor. Indeed, I am what you might almost describe as poverty-stricken.'

'Bah!' said Papa Nikos with infinite scorn. 'You poverty-stricken? It is well known that you are the richest man in the village. I don't see why *you* shouldn't offer the reward.'

'Yes, yes,' chorused the villagers. 'It's only right. After

all, he *is* the richest man in the village and he is the Mayor.'

'Yes,' said the Inspector, 'I think you are quite right.'

The affair of the Mayor's bitch had rankled with the Inspector and he had been waiting for a suitable opportunity to try to get his own back, and this seemed to be the ideal time.

'But, I tell you, I am a poor man,' moaned the Mayor.

'Then, perhaps soon you will be a poor man and not even a Mayor,' said Papa Nikos grimly.

'Yes,' said Papa Yorgo. 'I wonder if the Inspector would like to know the story of the sweet potatoes?'

The Mayor went white, for he had not realised that anybody knew about the big swindle he had pulled off the year before.

'I was going to say,' he said desperately, 'if only you would let me finish, that in spite of being a poor man, I am willing to offer a modest reward of, say, five hundred drachma.'

The villagers laughed derisively.

'That's not going to get our donkeys back,' they chorused.

'No,' agreed the Inspector. No, that's far too little. It'll have to be much more than that.'

'Well, say one thousand drachma,' suggested the Mayor with an effort.

'Fool,' said Papa Nikos scornfully. 'Do you think that if you had stolen donkeys worth 25,000 drachma you would come and give information as to their whereabouts for a paltry thousand drachma?'

'Yes,' said the Inspector, 'I am inclined to agree. It will have to be much more substantial than that.'

'Five thousand drachma,' said the Mayor, the sweat

running in rivulets down his fat face and into his walrus moustache.

'Make it twenty,' suggested somebody from the crowd.

'Yes, that's much more like it,' agreed the Inspector. 'That's a fairly nice, substantial sum.'

'Very well, then,' said the Mayor, taking out his handkerchief and mopping his brow. 'Twenty thousand drachma.'

A hum of approval ran through the crowd.

'Tell me,' Papa Nikos asked the Inspector. 'When this Communist comes to you with the information, what do you intend to do to him?'

'Why, give him the money, of course,' said the Inspector.

'But aren't you going to arrest him?' asked Papa Nikos surprisedly. 'After all, he is a Communist.'

'It is a well-known fact,' said the Inspector wisely, 'that when a Communist has money, he ceases to be a Communist. So there will therefore be no reason to arrest him.'

The villagers were much struck by this powerful piece of logic.

'Tell me,' asked Papa Yorgo, 'how are we going to let them know about the reward?'

They thought about it for some minutes.

'Posters,' said Mayor Oizus suddenly, smitten with the first original idea he'd had since gaining office. 'We will put up posters.'

'But where will we put them up?' asked Papa Yorgo.

'We should really scatter them like they did during the war,' said Papa Nikos.

'An aeroplane would be the answer,' mused the Inspector, 'or a helicopter, but it would take too long to get one sent from Athens. No, I suggest that we put them in all the places where the Communists are *likely* to see them.'

'But, where's that?' asked Papa Nikos. 'Normally we hang up posters in the village.'

'Out in the olive groves,' explained the Inspector, waving his hands, 'down in the vineyards and in the fields where they're lurking.'

'How are we going to get these posters?' asked the Mayor.

It was the Inspector's big moment. He drew himself up majestically.

'I,' he said, 'have a cousin in Melissa who owns a printing press and he will print them for you . . . free.'

The burst of applause and cries of 'Bravo!' from the crowd were almost deafening and the Inspector sat there smiling smugly, secure in the knowledge that he had once again won the approval of the villagers.

'What do we say on these posters?' inquired Papa Nikos. 'We can't address it to anybody, because we don't know who they are.'

'I have given that some thought,' said the Inspector proudly and he produced another piece of paper from his pocket.

'This,' he continued, writing busily, 'is what I suggest we put. "To whom it may concern – particularly Communists. We, the people of Kalanero, in return for receiving information as to the whereabouts of our donkeys, are willing to pay the sum of twenty thousand drachma."

'Signed,' he continued, ' "Mayor Oizus." Now I'll take this in to Melissa and get it printed. They should be ready by to-morrow.'

He drove off in the police car to the cheers of villagers

and they dispersed to their various houses, chattering animatedly. Only the Mayor had a despondent look. The children were breathless with excitement.

'Isn't it *wonderful!*' said Amanda, her eyes shining. 'We've saved you, Yani! We've saved you!'

'Don't speak too soon,' said David.

'Oh, you are such a pessimist,' said Amanda. 'Of *course* we've saved him. All he's got to do is to tell them where the donkeys are and he can claim the reward.'

'Do you think for one minute that they wouldn't think that he'd pinched the donkeys if he went to claim the reward?'

'That's true, Amanda,' said Yani, 'for all the village knows that Mayor Oizus is threatening me.'

'I don't think it matters,' said Amanda. 'We can claim the reward and then give it to Yani. I think the villagers'll be so glad to get their donkeys back that they won't care who took them.'

'Well, don't let's get too excited about it,' said David. 'I wouldn't trust that Mayor for all the tea in China. He might try and back out of it.'

'I don't think he would be able to do that,' said Yani. 'I think he's too frightened of what the villagers would do to him if he did that.'.

'Well, we'll wait and see,' said David.

The following morning the police car once more returned from Melissa and from the back of it, with great pride, the Inspector produced a huge pile of posters taste-fully printed in scarlet on a white ground, and with the sum of twenty thousand drachma written extra large (both in words and figures) in case, as he pointed out, it should be a Communist who could not read.

The posters were an immediate success. Apart from anything else, they were so pretty to look at. The Inspector's cousin was not a very expert printer and so the lines of writing went up and down like the waves of the sea, but everybody agreed that this enhanced rather than detracted from the charm of the posters and, in fact, as Mama Agathi pointed out, they were so beautiful it was really a shame to hang them up in places where only Communists could see them. The villagers all agreed, so they set one aside which they pinned up carefully on the café door. Then the posters were distributed with much arguing and shouting, for they were so beautiful that even those people of Kalanero who had no donkeys and therefore had had no donkeys stolen, wanted to have a poster.

The children watched with glee as the villagers spent the morning carefully and proudly tacking up their posters on olive trees, vine supports and to the little bamboo fences that divided all their fields. Mama Agathi was so entranced by her two posters that she even went to Mrs Finchberry-White and borrowed a feather duster so that she could go out periodically and dust them, to make sure not a speck of dust marred their pristine brilliance. Amanda and David were almost hysterical with laughter by the time they got back to the villa for lunch.

'Oh, there you are, dears,' said Mrs Finchberry-White. 'I was just coming to look for you. Lunch will be a little late. We had a slight accident over the soup. I asked Agathi to serve it and for some obscure reason she poured it down the sink. She was very upset, poor thing.'

The children made their way out on to the terrace where the General was standing squinting malevolently through his monocle at his latest masterpiece.

'Mother says lunch will be a little late,' reported Am-

anda. 'She says that for some obscure reason Mama
Agathi poured the soup down the sink.'

'The reason,' said the General, 'is not obscure at all.
It's just simply that your mother, with her gift for tongues,
told her to throw it away instead of to bring it out here,
with the not unnatural result that she poured it down the
sink.'

'Oh,' said Amanda, giggling, 'I didn't realise it was that.'

'By the way,' said the General, leaning forward and

adding a touch of colour to his picture, 'I trust you are
giving those donkeys enough to eat.'

Amanda and David, who had just spread-eagled themselves on the warm flagstones, sat up as though they had
been shot.

'What donkeys?' asked Amanda cautiously.

The General added another touch of colour to his
picture.

'Donkeys,' he said. 'You know, quadrupeds, beasts of
burden; those things with long ears that bray.'

David and Amanda glanced at each other.

'I . . . I don't know what you mean,' said Amanda.

'I mean,' said the General patiently, 'all the donkeys of Kalanero which you have got carefully hidden on Hesperides.'

The children looked at each other in horror.

'How on earth did you know about that?' asked Amanda.

The General put down his palette and brush, took out his pipe and lit it.

'I told you the other day,' he said, 'that I don't disclose my sources of information as a rule. However, on this particular occasion I will tell you. Coocos was my informant.'

'Coocos?' chorused the children incredulously. 'Coocos told you?'

'Yes,' said the General. 'He has kept me informed of the matter from the very start.'

'But, he couldn't have,' said Amanda. '*Not Coocos!* Why, he can't even talk.'

'On the contrary,' said the General, 'Coocos can talk very well. It is an impediment of speech, not of mind, that he suffers from. It's just that everybody is so impatient they won't stop to *let* him talk. Coocos loves talking, but nobody ever lets him.'

'Poor Coocos, 'said Amanda slowly, 'I'd never thought of that.'

'I, however,' continued the General, 'have the patience to listen to him and so, whenever he can, he comes up here and I paint and he talks. You needn't think, however, that he let you down by telling me. He was under the impression that I was master-minding the whole plot, as a matter of fact, since you had said something about asking my advice.'

'Oh, yes,' said Amanda, 'that was about the kidnapping.'

'Yes, I thought it was that,' said the General. 'However, I didn't disillusion him, but I received, with interest, a constant stream of reports from him as to how the plot was going.'

'But why didn't you stop us?' asked David.

'My dear David,' said the General, 'you are quite old enough and have a sufficient quantity of brain to be able to organise your own lives. If you wanted to get yourselves into trouble it was your affair, not mine. In any case, as you were doing it for the best possible motives, I saw absolutely no reason to interfere.'

'But then, what did you tell the Inspector?' asked Amanda.

'Ah,' said the General, puffing at his pipe, 'there I must say I *did* interfere slightly. It struck me that you had committed no grave criminal offence by stealing the donkeys, since you intended to return them. However, if you had sent a ransom note (which I presumed was going to be your next step) then I am afraid I would not have been able to save you from the wrath of the law. So I suggested to the Inspector that his best method was to offer a reward.'

'Father, you are clever!' said Amanda admiringly.

'I am frequently dazzled by my own brilliance,' said the General modestly.

'Well, what do you think we ought to do now?' asked Amanda.

'I would suggest that you wait until to-morrow,' said the General, 'discover the whereabouts of the donkeys and then claim the reward.'

He tapped out his pipe on the edge of the terrace and hummed a few bars of 'The Road to Mandalay' to himself.

'I might even,' he remarked, 'walk as far as the village square for the sake of seeing Oizus pay up. You see, I don't like him any more than you do and I happen to like Yani very much.'

CHAPTER 9

Payment

After lunch the children went down to have their last council of war with Yani.

'I really think,' said David as they made their way through the olive groves, 'that we should tick Coocos off.'

'You will do no such thing,' said Amanda indignantly. 'After all, he was only trying to help.'

'Yes, but he could have ruined everything if Father had put his foot down,' David pointed out.

'You are not to say anything to him,' said Amanda firmly. 'How would you like to go through life wanting to talk and nobody letting you?'

'All right,' said David resignedly, 'but that is just the sort of thing that makes first-class plans come unstuck.'

When they told Yani, he was as horrified as they had been, but he, too, sided with Amanda and agreed that they should say nothing to Coocos about the matter.

'Now,' said Amanda briskly, 'it's merely a question of claiming the reward. I suggest this evening would be a suitable time to discover the donkeys.'

'Now, let's get this quite clear,' said David. 'Yani must not be implicated in discovering the donkeys. If he is, the Mayor will know that he took part in pinching them. It's got to be done by us.'

'All right,' said Amanda. 'We'll swim across to Hesperides about four o'clock and discover them on the island. Surprise! Surprise!'

'Yes,' said David, 'because by the time we get back to the village with the news everyone will have had their siestas.'

'I wonder what their reactions are going to be?' mused Amanda.

'They'll be grateful beyond belief,' said Yani, chuckling. 'I don't think they ever realised before how much they needed their donkeys.'

'It's very unlikely that the Mayor is going to have twenty thousand drachma in his house,' observed David shrewdly, 'which means that he will have to go into Melissa for it, which means that we really can't get the reward until to-morrow.'

'Well, that's all right,' said Amanda. 'It doesn't matter whether we get it to-day or to-morrow.'

'No. But if he sleeps on it,' David pointed out, 'he might change his mind.'

'Well, he can't go into Melissa this evening,' said Yani, 'because the bank will be closed.'

David frowned and sighed.

'Yes. I can't see any other way of doing it,' he said. 'We'll just have to risk it.'

So that afternoon Yani and Coocos made it patently obvious to those villagers they met that they were going to have a siesta and, as it grew towards four o'clock, Amanda and David swam out through the warm blue water to Hesperides.

'You must admit,' said Amanda, shaking her wet hair and surveying the donkeys and the Mayor's little horse, 'that they look worlds better for their rest.'

'Yes, they do,' agreed David. 'In fact, I think it would be a good idea if this happened to them once a year.'

'What, you mean that they were brought out to Hesperides?' asked Amanda.

'Yes,' said David, 'a sort of holiday camp for donkeys.'

'It would be a good idea,' said Amanda, musingly, 'but I doubt whether we could get the villagers to adopt it.'

'Well,' said David, 'the thing for you to do is to swim back and rush up to the village. Round about now the Mayor will be awake and having his first cup of coffee and everyone else will be around too. Remember to make it as dramatic as you can, and don't for heaven's sake giggle.'

'I never giggle,' said Amanda austerely.

'You do, you giggle incessantly.'

'I *don't* giggle,' said Amanda. 'I laugh.'

'Well, whatever it is you do, don't do it,' said David.

So, after patting the furry rumps of the donkeys, Amanda ran down the stone steps from the church and plunged once more into the water. In order to give an air of authenticity to her part, she ran up the hill so that by the time she arrived in the village square, she was panting and exhausted.

As they had anticipated, Mayor Oizus, Papa Nikos and many other members of the village had just come from their siestas and had gathered round the tables at the café to discuss the burning question – when they would get information from the Communists as to the whereabouts of their donkeys. They were having a long and very complicated argument as to whether Communists could read or not when Amanda, perspiring profusely, came running into the village square.

'Mayor Oizus, Mayor Oizus,' she gasped, 'we've found them.' She flung herself panting and exhausted into the Mayor's lap.

'Found what, my golden one?' inquired the Mayor, startled.

It was obvious, however, from Amanda's incoherence that she was in no condition to answer him, so they plied her with glasses of wine and patted her back and made reassuring noises until she had regained her breath.

'The donkeys,' gulped Amanda at last. 'We've found them.'

The effect of this statement was electric. The Mayor rose to his feet spilling Amanda on to the floor and knocking over the table which held twelve ouzos and five cups of coffee.

'What?' he asked of the prostrate Amanda. 'You have found them?'

'Where? Where?' shouted Papa Nikos.

'Where have you found them?'

'Tell us, tell us quickly,' said Papa Yorgo.

Amanda, who liked to have her dramatic effects just as the villagers did, rose to her feet and leaned tragically on the upturned table.

'We have found them,' she repeated with a sob in her voice.

'They have been found!' shouted the Mayor. 'The donkeys have been found!'

Immediately the word was shouted from house to house and as if by magic the little square filled with villagers, all clamouring to know the truth.

'Where are they? Where are they?' asked Papa Nikos.

Amanda drew a long shuddering breath and lifted up her head nobly.

'David and I,' she said in a trembling voice, 'went for a swim this afternoon. We swam out to Hesperides. I think you all know it?'

There was a mutter of acknowledgment from the

villagers, hastily stilled so that they would not miss a word of her story.

'We climbed up the steps to the little terrace by the church,' Amanda continued, dragging out the story as long as she could.

'Yes, yes,' said the villagers, 'we know it, we know it.'

'And there,' said Amanda dramatically, 'to our astonishment, we found all the donkeys and the Mayor's little horse.'

'Saint Polycarpos preserve us,' shouted the Mayor. 'It is a miracle.'

'Were there any Communists with them?' asked Papa Yorgo.

'No,' said Amanda. 'No Communists and it seems as though they have been well looked after.'

'God be praised,' exclaimed Papa Nikos. 'If you two golden ones had run into the band of Communists, there is no knowing what they would have done to you.'

'But we ought to go and fetch them,' said the Mayor. 'Fetch them quickly before the Communists return.'

'Oh, don't worry,' said Amanda, 'I've left David there. He'll make sure that nothing happens.'

'The quicker we have them back the better,' said Papa Nikos.

'Down to the boats!' cried Papa Yorgo. 'Down to the boats to row across and fetch them!'

So the villagers of Kalanero, led by Amanda, ran and scrambled and tripped and fell down the stony hillside to the tiny port of Kalanero where the small fishing boats were anchored; it lay not far along the coast from Hesperides.

Here, complete pandemonium ensued; people got their anchor chains entwined, hit each other by accident with oars and, to Amanda's delight, the Mayor stepped into a boat that was just pushing off and fell into the shallow water. But eventually all the little fishing boats, over-loaded with eager villagers, were plying their way across the blue waters towards Hesperides. David, watching them approach the island, was vividly reminded of some pleasure boats that he had seen once at Swanage, bulging with holiday-makers being taken for a trip round the bay. The first boat to grind to a standstill on the shores of Hesperides was the one containing the extremely wet Mayor, and the others were not long in following. The villagers leaped ashore and ran up the steps where they paused dramatically to utter shouts of joy at the sight of their line of donkeys and the Mayor's little horse, all munching placidly.

'My little horse, my little horse,' wailed the Mayor, tears running down his cheeks.

He took the unprecedented step of actually throwing his arms round the neck of his biggest donkey and kissing it on the nose. Even Kouzos, who was not noted for his kindness to animals, was observed patting his donkeys surreptitiously, with a broad grin of pleasure on his face.

'But how did the Communists get them over here?' asked Papa Nikos when the excitement had died down a bit. 'They must have had a huge vessel to carry all these animals.'

'Oh, I shouldn't think so,' said Amanda. 'I should imagine that they swam them over.'

'*Can* donkeys swim?' asked Papa Nikos.

Amanda kept a straight face with difficulty.

'Ask the Mayor,' she replied.

'Yes, yes,' said the Mayor, 'they can swim. The day

when I fell off the bridge and these brave children saved me, my donkey was swimming like a fish.'

'I suggest that you take them back the same way,' said Amanda.

So the villagers, with infinite care, led their donkeys down the steps from the little church to the shore of Hesperides. But the holiday had obviously done the donkeys and the little horse too much good. They were even more reluctant to enter the water than they had been with the children, with the result that the beach resembled an uncontrolled rodeo, with villagers pushing and tugging and struggling to get their donkeys into the water. Mayor Oizus was kicked in the stomach by his little horse quite early in the proceedings and had to go and lie under a cypress tree to recover, leaving the job of getting his

beasts of burden into the sea to Amanda and David.
Eventually, however, the flotilla of little boats, with the
line of reluctant donkeys swimming behind, rowed back
to the mainland, where the rest of the villagers were
assembled on the jetty and gave them the sort of ovation
that is normally reserved for the maiden voyage of a large
ocean-going liner. Everybody had to pat and touch the
donkeys, everybody exclaimed on what a miracle it was
they had been discovered and how clever Amanda and
David had been. Finally, exhausted, they reached the
village square where the Mayor, in a fit of unprecedented
generosity, sent for a bottle of his own wine so that he
could toast Amanda and David. Solemnly the two children were toasted, then as they drank, cries of 'Bravo,'
'Beautiful children,' 'Golden ones,' and similar shouts of
endearment came from the villagers.

'You won't forget the reward, will you, Mayor Oizus?'
asked Amanda demurely, putting her empty glass on the
table. The Mayor, who had been wreathed in smiles,
started and almost dropped his glass.

'Reward?' he said. 'Reward?'

'You know,' said David, 'what you have written on the
posters. The reward of twenty thousand drachma.'

'Ah, *that*,' said the Mayor. 'Ah – um – yes, but that was
to get the Communists to show their hand. It was, as you
might call it, a ruse.'

'I told you so,' whispered David to Amanda.

'But Mayor Oizus,' said Amanda firmly, 'it says quite
clearly on the posters that you will pay twenty thousand
drachma to anybody who told you of the whereabouts of
your donkeys. We not only told you of their whereabouts,
but we showed you. So, therefore, we are entitled to the
reward.'

'But, my sweet ones,' said the Mayor, starting to perspire, 'it was all a joke.'

'It was not a joke,' said Papa Nikos grimly, 'and you know it.'

'Yes, yes,' said Papa Yorgø, 'it was not a joke.'

'You offered to pay the reward,' said Papa Nikos, 'and so you must pay it. These children have earned it.'

'Yes, they have indeed. They have indeed,' chorused the villagers.

'Well,' said the Mayor in desperation, 'if that's a unanimous decision, I suppose I'll have to, but I haven't got the money with me here. I shall have to go into Melissa and fetch it.'

'That's all right,' said Amanda sweetly. 'We'll come and collect it to-morrow afternoon at four o'clock.'

'Yes, yes,' echoed the villagers, 'at four o'clock.'

'At four o'clock,' agreed the Mayor dismally.

So the children, having been patted and hugged and kissed by the grateful villagers of Kalanero, made their way back to the villa.

'Well,' asked the General when they appeared on the terrace, 'how did it go?'

'It was splendid,' said Amanda. 'I wish you could have seen the Mayor fall into the water, it was even funnier than seeing him fall off the bridge.'

'Yes, I missed that,' said David gloomily.

'And then,' Amanda said, 'they were so excited at getting their donkeys back that the Mayor actually kissed his.'

'If people took more time in life to kiss donkeys,' observed the General, 'the world would be a better place.'

'They had a terrible time trying to get the donkeys to

swim back,' said David, 'and the Mayor's little horse kicked him in the stomach.'

'A retribution long overdue,' said the General with satisfaction.

'We got them all back,' said David, 'then we asked the Mayor about the reward.'

'Ah,' said the General, 'and what did he say?'

'Oh, he tried to pretend it was all a joke,' said Amanda indignantly.

'I told you he would,' said David. 'I wouldn't trust that man for anything.'

'Fortunately,' said Amanda, 'the villagers all backed us up and said we had earned the reward, so eventually the Mayor had to give in. We are going down to collect it to-morrow at four o'clock.'

'Masterly,' said the General with satisfaction. 'Quite masterly.'

'I am surprised at your approving of this,' said Amanda.

'Why should I disapprove?' inquired the General. 'It was a well-conceived plan, carefully carried out; it hurt nobody and it is going to do Yani a lot of good. I see absolutely no reason why I shouldn't approve of it.'

Amanda shrugged; the General's thought processes had always been and would always remain an enigma to his daughter.

'I shall come down myself,' said the General, 'and I shall bring your mother, too.'

'Where to, Henry?' inquired Mrs Finchberry-White, who had just appeared in a dazed sort of fashion on the terrace.

'Down to the village to watch Amanda and David getting their reward,' said the General.

'Reward?' said Mrs Finchberry-White. 'Reward for what?'

'I spent the entire morning,' said the General irritably, 'telling you on my leg drum, and I refuse to go over the whole thing again.'

'It's just that the villagers lost their donkeys,' explained Amanda hastily, 'and we found them and so we can claim the reward that they offered for them.'

'How very nice, dear,' said Mrs Finchberry-White. 'Have you seen that tiny little green orchid that grows down in the trees there? I've a very strong feeling that it isn't in my collection.'

The following morning the Mayor on his little horse trotted along the dusty road to Melissa and, though it seared his soul to do so, he drew twenty thousand drachma out of his account at the bank, counted it carefully and stowed it away in his wallet. Then he trotted sadly back to Kalanero.

At four o'clock there was not a single inhabitant of Kalanero (who was not too old or too young to be present) who was not assembled in the village square to watch the giving of the reward. The pleasure it gave the villagers was twofold. Firstly, because Amanda and David were such favourites in the village and secondly because the villagers were enchanted at the thought of the Mayor having to part with twenty thousand drachma. Major-General Finchberry-White and his wife walked down and stood on the outskirts of the crowd in the square and Amanda and David made their way forward to the café where the Mayor was seated behind a table covered, for this special occasion, with a white cloth. The Mayor, since he realised he was going to have to part with his money, decided to put the best possible face on things. And so, as

Amanda and David came to a halt in front of the table, he rose to his feet and made a little speech.

'People of Kalanero,' he said oratorically. 'It has long been the reputation of Melissa and in particular of the village of Kalanero, that they have always been eager to have strangers living in their midst and have been hospitable to them.'

'Quite right,' muttered Papa Yorgo.

'When these golden ones first came to live with us,' the Mayor continued, 'we took them instantly to our hearts. Brave, noble and modest aristocrats.'

A mutter of assent ran through the village square.

'During the time they have been here,' said the Mayor, 'they have done many wonderful deeds for us, the people of Kalanero, not least among these being the saving of my life when the bridge collapsed under me.'

He paused and drank a glass of water.

'Now,' he continued, throwing out his arms dramatically, 'they have, through their astuteness and courage, saved the entire village of Kalanero by recovering for us our donkeys and my little horse.'

'I do wish he would shut up,' said David, who was getting increasingly embarrassed.

'Poor man, let him have his fun,' whispered Amanda.

'As you all know,' said the Mayor, 'I offered a reward for the recovery of the donkeys and being a man of my word, I intend to give that reward now to these two wonderful children.'

With a flourish he pulled his wallet out of his pocket and proceeded with great care to count out two piles of hundred-drachma notes. You could hear every villager counting with the Mayor as he put the notes down. He slapped the final note on the table and threw his arms out.

'Twenty thousand drachma,' he cried in a shaking voice.
'Twenty thousand drachma which I am paying for the
recovery of our donkeys by the two foreigners in Melissa
that we love most.'

The cheers of the crowd were deafening.

'Go on,' muttered David, 'you pick up the money.'

'No, you do it,' said Amanda, who was feeling as guilty
as David.

'Well, let's do it together,' said David as a compromise.

So they both stepped forward and each picked up their
pile of ten thousand drachma. Instantly silence settled on
the little square and it was obvious that the villagers expected the children to reply in some way to the Mayor's
speech. Amanda glanced at David, but he was red-faced
and tongue-tied, so Amanda cleared her throat and began.

'People of Kalanero,' she said. 'To-day we have been
greatly honoured by Mayor Oizus inasmuch as he is paying us the reward for the discovery of your donkeys. Now,
we know that there are many of you here who are poor,
who are much poorer than us, for example, and so I and
my brother feel that it would be unfair to take this money.'

The Mayor started at this and a faint feeling of hope
crept over him.

'So, my brother and I,' Amanda continued, 'have discussed what would be the best thing to do. You know that
all the people of Kalanero are our friends, but one of our
particular friends is Yani Panioti.'

She beckoned to Yani, who was in the crowd, and he
came forward and joined the children by the table.

'As you know,' said Amanda, 'Yani's father died last
year and unfortunately he died in debt.'

'Yes, yes,' murmured the villagers, 'we know that.'

'So my brother and I,' said Amanda, 'have decided to

give this money to Yani so that he may repay his father's debts.'

The cries of 'Bravo,' 'What generosity,' and other similar statements were overwhelming. Amanda and David solemnly handed the money over to Yani. Yani, with tears in his eyes, kissed David on both cheeks and to the delight of the villagers he kissed Amanda full on the mouth. Then he turned to the Mayor.

'Mayor Oizus,' he said, 'here is the eighteen thousand drachma that my father owed you. The entire village is witness to the fact that I am now paying up his debt in full.'

He placed the sheaf of notes carefully in front of the Mayor. Again the shouts of 'Bravo' were deafening, but the Mayor, instead of being pleased at having most of his money returned to him, appeared to be undergoing a strange change. His normally pale, cheese-coloured face had suddenly become suffused with blood and his eyes bulged.

'*You* did it,' he shouted, suddenly getting to his feet and pointing a shaking finger at Amanda, David and Yani. '*You* did it.'

The villagers fell silent. This was a new twist to the plot which they had not anticipated.

'*They* took the donkeys,' shouted the Mayor, almost apoplectic with rage. '*They* took the donkeys so that they could claim the reward so that they could give it to Yani Panioti and deprive me of my legal right to his land. *They* are the "Communists" that we have all been searching for.'

The villagers, round-eyed, looked at the children. It took a moment or so for the Mayor's words to penetrate, but when they did, and the villagers grasped their implication, the whole gorgeousness of the situation dawned upon them. The Mayor had been treated ignominiously, had been forced to part with twenty thousand drachma, and Yani Panioti had been saved, and all by the cleverness of their English children. It was Papa Nikos who started it, for as soon as the full beauty of the situation dawned on him, he uttered a bellow of laughter that could have been heard half a mile away. Any other crowd would have been indignant at what the children had done, but these were Melissiots and they thought differently. All the villagers started to laugh and they laughed and laughed and laughed. The Mayor shouted and raved for a time, and then gave up in despair because he could not make himself heard for the great waves of laughter.

And so the three children, with something very much approaching a swagger, made their way through the village square, through the villagers, some of whom were laughing so much that they could hardly stand, and wended their way up to the villa.

The Fib and other stories

GEORGE LAYTON

I was sick of Gordon Barraclough: sick of his bullying and his shouting, and his crawling round Mr Melrose, sick of him being a good footballer and going on about my old football gear. So I told him it had belonged to my uncle, who'd scored thousands of goals – because my uncle was Bobby Charlton! That was the fib. Then Bobby Charlton turned up as the surprise celebrity to switch on the Christmas lights outside the town hall. 'You're in for it now,' said Gordon, 'I told him you said he's your uncle.' I looked up at Bobby Charlton. He looked down at me. If only the earth would open and swallow me up . . .

Based on George Layton's own childhood, here are ten short, funny stories that come straight to the point on many important issues of adolescent life, such as school, girlfriends, football, and the problems of keeping in with your mates and getting round mum.

The Phantom Tollbooth

Norton Juster

'It seems to me that almost everything is a waste of time,' Milo remarks as he walks dejectedly home from school. But his glumness soon turns to surprise when he unwraps a mysterious package marked *One Genuine Phantom Tollbooth*.

Once through the Phantom Tollbooth, Milo has no more time to be bored for before him lies the strange land of the Kingdom of Wisdom and a series of even stranger adventures.

'The story is always charmingly inventive – Jules Feiffer's drawings splendidly catch the spirit of it – and in some families I think it could become a well-thumbed classic.'

Guardian

The Size Spies
JAN NEEDLE

It's not every day the cat catches a mouse and puts it in your boot.

It's not every day the cuckoo clock pinches your breakfast sausage.

It's not every day the dog eats your comic and blows a fuse.

To George and Cynthia, stuck in a dilapidated farm-house out on the Yorkshire Moors with a totally mad professor and a huge (not to say tiny) problem, these little things just about put the tin lid on it. Something's got to happen, and it's got to happen NOW!

Well it does. Before they know exactly what's hit them, George and Cynthia are in the thick of an absolutely lunatic adventure, involving spies, dangerous inventions, two peculiar boys called Jugears and Mophead, a set of stolen parents and a *very* near escape at London Airport. Before much longer they've got themselves into a right old mess.

A very funny, exciting tale illustrated with zany line drawings by Roy Bentley.